"Don't run from me, Elizabeth."

That was the first time he'd used her name, and it sent shivers of longing down her spine. It sounded so good on his lips. "I'm not running, Rand. But you need to keep your mind on learning right now. I'm a therapist, not a girlfriend. And I just don't think—"

"Good. Don't think," he whispered. "I've been wanting to do this ever since you first walked into my life."

Rand pulled her forward and touched her hair. His left hand traced her face, looking at her as only he could, following her high cheekbones, her eyes, brushing her eyelashes before touching her nose. Finally his hand cupped her cheek. "You're beautiful. I only wish I could see you."

"But you did," she whispered, stepping back. "You saw me in your own way."

CHERYL WOLVERTON

Growing up in a small military town in Oklahoma where she used to make up stories with her next-door neighbor, Cheryl says she's always written but never dreamed of having anything published. But after years of writing her own Sunday school material in the different churches where she's taught young children, and wanting to see more happy endings, she decided to give it a try, and found herself unable to stop. *A Matter of Trust* is Cheryl's first published work and is a story dear to her heart.

Seeing so many people hurting, afraid to reach out and accept God's forgiveness, inspired her to begin writing stories about God's love and forgiveness in romances, because, she says, "We can't truly have happily ever after, if we don't have that happily ever after relationship with God, too."

Cheryl now lives in a small Louisiana town and has been happily married for fifteen years. She has two wonderful children who think it's cool to have a "writing mama." Cheryl would love to hear from her readers. You can write to her at P.O. Box 207, Slaughter, LA 70777.

A MATTER OF TRUST

Cheryl Wolverton

Love Inspired

Published by Steeple Hill Books™

STEEPLE HILL BOOKS

Steeple
Hill™

ISBN 0-373-87011-6

A MATTER OF TRUST

"Come unto me all ye who labor and are heavy laden, and I will give you rest.
Take my yoke upon you, and learn of me; for I am meek and lowly in heart: and ye shall find rest unto your souls."

—*Matthew* 11:28-29

Acknowledgments

Thanks to my critique partner, Yvonne Grapes, as well as my GEnie and Birt friends! Thanks, Sharon Gillenwater, for her gentle words and suggestions. And to my own "Phil-ton" a.k.a. Phil Hayward—a great friend. Especially thanks to my husband, Steve, and two children, Christina and Jeremiah, for all the chicken jokes!

And thanks to my mom, Helen, and in memory of my dad, Leo Weaver, who always believed in me. I love you.

Prologue

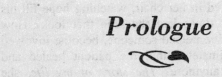

"**H**e's been through six nurses already. He's my *twin!*" Max Stevens told her, as if that explained the raw emotions on his face. "I can't leave my brother like this." He paused. His eyes searched the woman in front of him, determination mixed with desperation in his gaze. "I've heard you're different. You have a higher success rate in cases like this. You're my last hope."

Elizabeth Jefferson stared at the thirty-two-year-old man in front of her. His dark, rakish good looks concealed neither his grief nor the pleading in his eyes.

His last hope. Everyone had heard about the tragedy that had struck rich industrialist Rand Stevens, the accident that killed his wife and left him—

"I'll pay you double your usual fees. You'll have to—" he coughed uncomfortably "—live in," he finished.

Elizabeth raised an eyebrow. Most men were so worldly minded. She was surprised by how uncomfortable he seemed. She folded her hands on top of a neat stack of papers lying on her desk and leaned slightly forward. "I usually do live in for the first few weeks or so, depending upon the patient's progress. I also have full responsibility for that patient, what time he eats, what time he works on his therapy, everything."

"That's what they all say," Max muttered, then flushed. "Actually, Rand hasn't been very receptive to the idea of help."

Elizabeth relaxed in her chair, watching hope fill his eyes. How many times had she seen that look? How many times had she helped someone, become involved in their life, intimately, until the patient healed and didn't need her anymore? *The story of my life,* she thought cynically. But this man was different. His family drew publicity like some of her doctors wrote prescriptions—by the pad full. Treating Rand Stevens would mean possible media coverage. Nothing concerning the famous widowed millionaire would stay behind the scenes very long. Could she afford to risk that? What if Michael picked up a magazine or saw a news story about Rand and his therapy and found out where she was?

His eye is on the sparrow, Elizabeth, a tiny voice whispered.

She shuddered.

Have faith.

She sighed. *Well, Lord?* she questioned. *What am I going to do? Should I take the job?*

But she already knew the answer. And with that acceptance, a peace flooded her.

Looking into the battle-weary eyes of Max Stevens, she asked, "When do I start?"

Chapter One

"Sarah! Sarah, where are you?"

The tinkling of a bell, followed by a dull thud when the object hit a wall, greeted Elizabeth Jefferson as she entered the foyer of the large multilevel house.

She stepped aside so the butler and driver could sidle past with her luggage. Max, who had been hurrying toward the stairs, turned to her, relief written plainly on his weary features. "It's one of his bad days. He's, uh, he's been like this all morning," he said, as if apologizing for what she'd heard. Of course, he didn't know she'd heard a lot worse, Elizabeth thought.

"Sarah! Get up here. I want hot coffee, not this swill you served me!"

The shout came from somewhere near the back of the house, yet it was easily audible from where she stood. Another crash followed, a breaking cup, she surmised, from the shattering sound.

"Where is he?" she asked, deciding there was never a better time than the present to meet her new patient.

"Upstairs in bed."

They were crossing the middle of a very modern living room decorated in white and glass, but at that statement, Elizabeth paused. "Is it Mr. Stevens's custom to eat breakfast in bed?" she asked, afraid she already knew the answer.

"Oh, no, Miss Jefferson. Well, that is, until...until after the—"

"After the accident?"

He nodded and then proceeded to drag a hand down his face, which was already etched with a weariness that few men should ever have to wear. "We usually don't talk about *that* here, in front of Rand."

"I see." And she did. It wasn't at all unusual for a family to suddenly become very protective of one of their own when something disastrous happened. Many times that made her job all that much harder. "We're agreed I am to have full responsibility for Mr. Stevens?" she asked, more to reinforce it in Max's mind than ask permission. She wouldn't have taken the job if he'd not agreed to her terms.

"Yes. Of course."

"Good. Now, I'll need a room as close to his as possible. Just have my luggage put there—"

The scowl on Max's face gave her pause.

"And why do you need to be that close?"

She forced herself not to bristle. "I need him dependent on me, no other reason."

She saw suspicion in his eyes and wondered if he thought she was going to try to crawl into his... A dull red flush crept up her cheeks. "No other purpose, I assure you."

Seeing her reaction, Max sighed. "I hope not, but two of the last nurses... Look, I'm sorry, but he's my brother and very vulnerable—"

"Sarah!"

Elizabeth gave Max a sardonic look. "I assume Sarah is the cook?" At his nod, she continued briskly. "Well, tell her she's to take no more orders from Rand until I give her the okay."

She started toward the stairs just in time to intercept a middle-aged, harried woman who had rushed into the room carrying a tray of food. Savory aromas of eggs, bacon, biscuits and gravy drifted to her nostrils. "Don't worry about introductions. I think this should be a one-on-one," she said over her shoulder as she took the tray and kept walking.

Max looked a little concerned and stepped forward. "Are you sure?"

"Absolutely."

"But you don't know where he is."

She smiled. "I'll follow the bellows."

As if on cue, Rand roared, "Sarah!"

Please, Lord, help me, guide me in these next few minutes to make the right impression.

She continued up the staircase and down the hall until the bottom floor disappeared from sight. The hall was long, extending in both directions, and she realized that the rooms must be huge since there were so few doors. She guessed the upstairs to have three bedrooms on this end of the house, leaving probably three on the other end. Hearing a noise, she paused and watched as the butler and driver slipped past. Their footsteps made no sound on the plush tan carpet. They paused in front of the last door on the right, casting a quick glance at the opened door on the left before entering the other room with her luggage.

Bingo.

She'd found Rand Stevens.

She finished the quick trek to the last room, but paused to study the patient's surroundings before entering.

The room was spacious. It included a sofa and chairs with a TV, VCR and phone. The end tables and entertainment center were cherry wood Queen Anne furniture. Thick opulent curtains, no less decadent than the matching mahogany carpet, hung at the window and French doors. The doors evidently led to a part of the balcony she'd glimpsed on the long ride up the driveway.

From the open door on the right—the left one was closed—she heard someone mutter.

Her patient.

That must be his bedroom, and the other door led to an office or gym, she would bet. She'd been in many houses like this in the past five years, after her reputation had spread in the elite circles of medicine. Still, this was more luxurious than most, and had more notoriety attached.

She silently crossed the carpet and stopped dead at the sight that met her eyes.

The room looked like war-torn territory—the loser's side. Clothes were tossed everywhere. Shattered china was lying near her feet. Glancing at the wall, she saw the remains of fresh eggs and coffee drying on the pale blue print paper.

"Who's there?"

Her attention jerked past the armoire, the bookcases and bedside table to the huge king-size bed.

Her breath caught.

Rand Stevens was purported to be a mirror image of Max. And she had to admit, he did look like him. Except as he sat there with his sheet and blankets twisted about his lower body, she could tell that he weighed at least twenty pounds less than his twin. Since he wore no shirt, she could see the ugly red scars, from the broken ribs, she guessed, as well as from the removal of a spleen, that cut across his torso. He was still muscular, but not nearly as healthy looking as Max. Her heart broke. His face was haggard, and dark circles under his eyes attested to the many nights of tortured sleep that Max had mentioned.

"Answer me! Sarah, is that you?"

Elizabeth released her breath. "No. It's not." She strolled into the room, tray in hand. "I'm Elizabeth Jefferson, your new nurse."

"My new... *Max!* Get in here! Where are you?"

Elizabeth set the tray on the table, but instead of feeding him, she picked up a piece of bacon and munched on it.

He had just opened his mouth to bellow again when he heard the crunch. He paused. "What are you doing?" Sniffing, he turned toward where she was. An incredulous look on his face, he demanded, "Is that my breakfast?" Then before she could answer, he inquired, shocked, "Are you *eating* my breakfast?"

"Most people call me Elizabeth," she said, as if she hadn't heard him, although there was a clear note of amusement in her voice. "But you can call me Beth, or even Jeff. I answer to most anything." Seating herself, she reached for another piece of bacon, only to pause. "Hey, why'd the chicken cross the road?"

She saw a dumbfounded look on his face. "What?"

She laughed before popping the last of the bacon in her mouth and then starting on the eggs. "Wrong! The real answer was to get away from the colonel."

"What the *devil* are you talking about?"

"Boy, it sure is messy in here. Doesn't anyone ever

clean?'' She slurped the coffee. "You know, I usually don't like coffee, but this is good. Must be all that real cream. I usually don't drink cream. I don't want to put on too much extra weight—''

"You're drinking *my* coffee? Are you crazy, lady? Give me my tray!''

"Uh-uh,'' she answered, scraping the tray across the table as she pulled it closer to her. His mouth dropped open in stunned amazement at the sound of her defiance, but she didn't let that bother her. "I already started—well, actually, I'm done except for the orange juice.''

She picked up the glass and drained it. "There. Now, lunch will be at eleven-thirty—''

"You going to eat that, too?'' he asked nastily, his face red and his hands clenched with anger.

"Of course. Only down in the dining room. *With you.*''

A sudden flash of fear crossed Rand's face before absolute fury replaced it. "I don't have to do what you say, lady. As a matter of fact, you're fired.''

"Uh-uh,'' she repeated, before standing. "Your brother hired me, not you.''

"I'll see he fires you.''

"Too late. He paid me one month, in advance, double wages. I'm not giving it back and I wouldn't feel right not fulfilling my obligation. Besides, I already spent most of it. Smell the perfume?'' She waved her hands by her neck. leaning forward, knowing he might not be able to see her but he would sense her movement and the movement of the air about him with the keen senses he had developed since the accident.

"Now, I just stopped by to meet you. I need to go unpack. I'll be back at eleven-thirty to go to lunch with you.''

"I won't go," he snarled, and she could hear the pain mingled with his anger.

"Then you won't eat." She picked up the tray.

"Hey, what about my breakfast?"

She paused by the door. "You already had yours, the remains of which are still on the wall."

"Sarah!"

"And don't call for her anymore. I've already ordered the staff not to bring you anything unless I approve it first, so it won't do any good to badger her to death."

"What gives you the right?" Rand roared and threw off the covers. He groped for the bedside table, found it and stood, keeping in contact with it as if it was his lifeline.

"I don't leave this room. I'm—"

He stopped, and Elizabeth finished. "Blind, Mr. Stevens. I know. But you're not crippled. I'll be back in two hours."

Leaving the room, she heard the vicious muttering of Rand Stevens just before the bedside clock hit the wall.

But if she thought her battle over, she was wrong, for twin brother Max was waiting outside in the hallway and his angry countenance told her he'd heard everything that had just transpired.

Dear Father, now what?

Chapter Two

◥

She had barely pulled the door closed before Max demanded, "Just what the devil do you think you're doing tormenting my brother that way? If you were hungry you could have eaten before you'd gone up! I've never seen—"

He stopped, his jaw dropping in astonishment when Elizabeth ignored him and crossed to her room. How dare she walk off! Then she motioned for him to come in.

His shock only momentarily blunted his anger. By the time her door was closed, he opened his mouth to light into her. But she forestalled him by throwing her earlier words, and his promise, back at him. "Did you not tell me I had absolute authority with your brother?"

"Well, yes, but—"

"Then please don't say anything against me again within his hearing. Rand would enjoy knowing you and I were at odds. He's furious with me right now—"

"As he should be. I can't believe—"

"Please, Mr. Stevens, let me explain."

Years of managing employees and executives of the giant financial empire he and his brother owned had taught Max patience. But right now it seemed next to impossible to exhibit it. And he knew it was because he was emotionally involved in this situation. He and Rand shared a special empathy. When Rand was upset, he was upset, when Rand grieved, he grieved. And sometimes it was hard to filter out those emotions and not let them control him. That's what came from being a twin, he imagined. And with that close relationship there was a protectiveness that many couldn't understand. Still, if Elizabeth Jefferson wanted to explain, he could at least allow her that. So with much difficulty Max reined in his anger and said, "Fine. Go ahead and explain, if you can. But it had better be a *very* good explanation if you're going to justify your harsh behavior toward my brother."

"Simple. In a way," she added. "Rand has been difficult to live with, has he not?" At Max's nod, she continued. "And everyone has allowed it because he's gone through such a hard time."

"But—"

"Let me finish," she said quietly but determinedly. "He needs something different, someone to take over, help him escape out of his fear and guide him into wanting to learn."

"And you think you're that person?" Max asked sarcastically, though he was beginning to calm down.

"Well, nothing else has worked. So why not give him a reason to get well? He lost his wife while he was driving—"

"It wasn't his fault," Max said defensively. "It was raining and the other driver was drunk. He swerved to avoid him and lost control of the car."

"I didn't say it was his fault. But that doesn't stop him from blaming himself, hating himself for what happened. Have you ever wondered if maybe he just doesn't want to try because he's so wrapped up in his own bitterness?"

Max suddenly had an idea where she was going. "And you intend to get his mind off what happened by making him take his anger out on you? That's crazy."

"Actually, it usually works." She grinned cheekily. "By eating his breakfast—by the way, I had already eaten—I showed him how infantile his act of throwing the other tray was, and let him know he won't get away with it again. Of course he's mad. He's had everything he wanted in the months since he's left the hospital, and he won't like someone coming in disturbing his solitude—or at least that's what he's showing us right now. Let me ask you something, Mr. Stevens. How often does your brother get out of bed?"

Max's shoulders drooped. "As far as anyone knows, only to go to the bathroom, and then he insists on help."

She smiled gently. "Do you know he got out of bed a minute ago, when he was trying to fire me? That takes a lot of courage. And by standing, he showed that he was attempting an authoritative stance in the situation. I was very surprised. I think maybe your brother is more than ready to continue on with life, but just doesn't know how to get out of the grave he's dug himself in."

For the first time hope flickered inside Max. "Do you think so, Ms.—"

"Please, call me Elizabeth."

"Do you really think it possible, Elizabeth?"

She shrugged. "I don't know. But I plan on trying my hardest to get him up and around. It's going to take work. He's going to have to totally relearn everything.

I'll be teaching the staff, as well, about moving things around. That's something everyone will have to learn. Mr. Stevens needs stability and normalcy in the environment he lives in, especially when he first starts getting out. Right now, considering how messy his room is, I would prefer him to stay in bed. If he tripped it could set him back months.''

Max flushed. ''He doesn't want anyone cleaning his room.''

''I understand. That's the only area he feels in control of, but in this case, his desires must be tempered with good sense.''

Max nodded. ''I had no idea...'' He trailed off, embarrassed suddenly that he had taken her to task a moment ago. ''I owe you an apology.''

''Nonsense,'' she replied, flushing a little. ''You'd be surprised how relatives react to my methods. Some never get over it. I'm just glad you're trying to understand. It's hard when you love someone and you have to watch them go through more pain than they've already experienced. Just think of it like...''

She paused, tapping her chin before she came up with an idea. He could see it spread across her face like the sun breaking through the clouds.

''When you break a leg you have to go through therapy—if it's a bad break—and sometimes that therapy can be very painful before you get better. Well, this is like that. Except that it's emotional therapy. It's going to hurt for awhile, but he'll come out a lot stronger. You know, it's darkest before the dawn, so to speak.''

''A Bible verse?'' he asked, surprised that this young woman would quote him the Bible.

She flushed. ''Yes. One of my favorites, as a matter of fact.''

He smiled and silently thanked God. Out of all the women who had been in the house, this was the first one who had quoted God's word to him, and he couldn't believe this wasn't an answer to his prayer. Peace flowed through him, and he knew without a doubt that his brother was finally going to get better. He sent a silent thank-you heavenward even as a smile spread across his face. "You do whatever you need and know that I'll back you one hundred percent."

Elizabeth's eyes widened. "Why, thank you."

"No problem." With a reassuring smile, Max left the room.

Elizabeth sank down on the side of her bed and sighed heavily. The first meeting was always the worst. But she had fared pretty well, she thought. Glancing in the mirror across the room she noted ruefully her short red hair was still attached to her head. Rand Stevens could have tried to pull it out, just like the last patient had. Running her right hand through the short, straight strands, she admitted that Rand Stevens did not seem the hair-pulling type. However, she wasn't sure yet exactly what type he was.

Rand, she knew from her bio on him, was used to a position of power. He was a go-getter, always striving for success, insisting on being the best at everything he did. She wanted to somehow tap into that and get him going in the right direction. She knew she could, with God's help. She just had to allow God to show her the way.

Would it be through her sense of humor? Most of her patients found her jokes outrageous or amusing—after awhile. Elizabeth was a natural cutup and she passed along her humorous view of the world to her patients as she worked with them. Rand was going to be more difficult, she feared.

She opened her suitcase and unpacked her clothes, hanging them in the solid cherry wood armoire as she went along.

He had certainly thrown her for a loop when she'd entered his room. Her insides had quivered and her hands shook as though she had palsy. Never had she been that nervous around a patient before. And when he'd come out of the bed...

She closed her empty suitcase, went to the small case by the vanity and began to unpack it.

Elizabeth had reacted to him on a purely feminine level, which surprised her. She *never* reacted to a man on that level. She had learned her lesson with Michael. After that very painful and disastrous relationship, she had decided that God was the only support she needed in her life. It had taken years, but she had finally healed after her ex-fiancé, even if the fear wasn't completely gone. There was always the chance he would locate her again. She remembered his calls and threats that he would find her and see she was paid back for what he considered her defection from their relationship. He didn't believe she had the right to break it off, and according to him, she was still his property.

She shuddered. He had found her in two different cities. The first time she'd picked up and left before he'd caught her alone. The second time he'd been arrested for stalking her. After the court appearance she had packed up and moved. Michael had been forced to serve a six-month sentence, but she still wanted to move somewhere new, where he wouldn't find her. She knew if he found her it would only be a matter of time before he turned violent again. She had eventually settled here, in Louisiana, certain he wouldn't check the South for her when he was freed. Evidently he hadn't, for that had been three years ago.

Her life was going forward again. Rarely did she look back. She had found a terrific church, with wonderful people. She lived in a nice little apartment in a nice area of Baton Rouge. She did very well with her job. People from all over the Southern states called her in when they needed help. Rich, poor, it didn't matter. If the doctors needed her, she usually went. The only drawback to her job was the fear that one day her picture was going to turn up in a paper and Michael would see it.

But oddly, that was not what was bothering her at the moment. Instead, it was her patient, Rand Stevens, who captured her thoughts and held them.

Rand Stevens was blind, angry and filled with bitterness. He was just like any other patient she had worked with in the past, expect for one small detail—he set her heart to hammering like she was going into cardiac arrest.

She had everything arranged just the way she wanted it. She didn't need a handsome man cluttering her thoughts! Not now, not when she was so happy again and everything was finally back to normal in her life. "God, take these feelings away," she whispered as she finished unpacking the small suitcase. "I can't afford to feel this!"

Closing her suitcase, she looked at her face and wished she was prettier. Her blue eyes were just average, she imagined, except she was told they flashed when she was angry. She had high cheekbones and a long face. That was one reason she wore her hair short. It made her face look rounder, but she knew her face was long, even if everyone else told her it was gorgeous. She wondered what Rand would see....

Jerking herself from that thought, she reminded herself that was why she was here. Pulling a folder out of her briefcase, which was next to the chair, she laid it on her vanity. Opening it to the brief summary, she began to read. "Thirty-two-year-old male who had severe trauma to the chest and head. Some possible optical nerve damage. Is purported to have occasional flashes of light and headaches. A small chance remains that vision could return. Refuses any more surgery. Doctor wonders if it might be psychosomatic but Rand refuses any more doctors' examinations as of six months ago. Doctor fears guilt over wife's death is keeping the patient from allowing himself to heal emotionally. Patient is moody, unresponsive."

She thought of his responses to her and decided he had definitely moved to a more active role. "Refuses to take calls or allow anyone in his room."

Well, that was still true. "Patient needs exercise and psychological evaluation."

"Well, you may be right there, buddy," Elizabeth stated, closing the folder. "I will admit it would help if Rand Stevens would open up and talk to someone about the accident. But unfortunately, I doubt I'm the one he's going to want to confide in, so that part of his healing will have to wait. We're going to have to work on his physical well-being first." Even as she said it, she had a strange feeling she was wrong.

Dropping her head onto her hand, she sighed. "I don't suppose, Father, that You have his brother in mind for that talk? I don't know that I'm up to helping this man emotionally. He's too disturbing, too...I dunno. Maybe You could... Never mind. I know better than to try to bargain. Just remember, please, that I'm not sure I can handle this.''

I'd never put more on you than you could bear. My yoke is easy, My burden is light. The scripture verse popped into her mind.

"Yeah, that's true," Elizabeth mused. "But with *this* man? He makes me nervous. I don't know why. And he's so handsome, even if he is too skinny!"

Done talking to her Father for the moment, she stood. She still needed to unpack her bathroom things and then go talk to the cook about preparing the meals for Rand Stevens. They had to be prepared on the plate a certain way. And she wanted to talk to the housekeeper about cleaning Rand's room at the first opportunity, as well as arranging things in the house, and then finally she wanted to warn Max that the first meal and quite possibly even more this week would be just her and Rand. She wouldn't force her patient into an uncomfortable situation. Therefore she needed to judge him, see just how strong he would be. It was possible it might work better with Max there. But first she'd have to see for herself how Rand handled going downstairs with her.

She didn't want to hurt Max, but was almost certain Rand would refuse to eat if anyone else was present until he convinced himself he could make it downstairs without killing himself.

And if she was truthful, she was also afraid Max might interfere—unintentionally—with her if he felt Rand's tension.

Heading toward the bathroom, she prayed she was making the right decisions and that Rand would be ready in an hour to go downstairs with her.

Elizabeth tapped a perfunctory knock on Rand's door before entering. "Hey, why'd the chicken cross the road?'' she called out as she crossed the main room toward his bedroom.

Stopping at the door, she saw him sitting on the bed, arms crossed, his face turned toward the window. ''No answer, huh? You catch on fast.''

''You already asked that,'' he muttered, although she was certain he hadn't meant to answer at all.

She grinned. ''Wrong.'' She sang it out in a sweet, cajoling voice. ''To get to the other side.''

His head turned just a little, but she saw it. It was like he'd wanted to do a double take. She giggled. ''I've got hundreds of them.''

No groan—yet. Oh, well…she didn't expect miracles the first day. ''I'm ready to go downstairs. I wasn't sure if you dressed or not, so I put on a mint green linen pants set. Goes good with my red hair, though I prefer to wear pink.''

She saw him frowning. ''You're right. Pink looks awful on me. But I *like* it. Anyway, since you're still in your pajama bottoms, I assume I could have kept on my jeans.''

She crossed the room, making sure there was a cleared path from the bed to the door. ''Are you ready for lunch?''

Finally, Rand turned his head in her direction. His face showed anger simmering barely beneath the surface, just waiting for an excuse to explode. Oh, he wanted to blast her, but he wouldn't, until she gave him a reason. However, arguing didn't fall in that category.

''I told you, I don't leave this room. I want my lunch delivered here,'' he said mulishly.

She grinned but did her best to keep the smile out of

her voice. Instead, she said breezily, "'Fraid not. Lunch is downstairs or nowhere."

"I'm not leaving this room. So why don't you go downstairs and just eat my lunch right along with yours, Ms. Jefferson."

"Nah, I can wait. I had a good breakfast, remember? Besides, if you're not hungry, there's a lot of other things I need to do."

She turned and surveyed his room. "Uh-huh. A lot of other things."

Concern tinged his voice. "What are you talking about?"

"Well, for starters, I need to clean your room. I'm liable to trip over something in this mess."

"Leave my room alone!"

Elizabeth paused at the foot of his bed, where she'd scooped up some clothes that were scattered there. "I don't have anything else to do until one o'clock. That's when your training is supposed to begin. I might as well do this now, instead of later."

"I like my room the way it is."

He sounded like a little boy, but Elizabeth knew better. This was a full-grown man, used to having his way. She'd give him a compromise. "You can either go downstairs, or I'll stay in here for the next hour and clean this room."

"This is *my* room."

"Yes, it is, Mr. Stevens. But *I'm* your therapist. I will be making the decisions for you until you can make them on your own."

"I am completely capable of making decisions right now."

"Let me rephrase that. Until you are capable of making logical decisions, based on facts and not emotions."

Yep, that did it. He was furious. She'd pricked his pride. His hands clenched and unclenched and his face turned red. It was fascinating watching him as he brought his temper under control. This man would be a wonder in business negotiations. "Fine. I'll go downstairs. I hope you don't mind how I'm dressed." The last was said in an I-don't-care-if-you-do voice.

"Not at all. Do you want your robe?"

"No. This is my house. I can dress as I please."

"Of course you can."

"Stop agreeing with me."

Rand, who was halfway out of bed, paused. She could see consternation written plainly across his face. She grinned. "Why, Mr. Stevens," she drawled. "I do believe you want to fight."

"I want you gone," he grumbled and stood. Slowly, he let go of the bedside table and his hands went out in front of him. Immediately, Elizabeth's joking was set aside. "Ten steps straight ahead and you'll be next to me."

He paused, and his features tightened. "I don't need a guide."

She didn't argue. Instead, she said, "But since I'm learning this house, too, you might as well let me practice it on you."

"Does that line work on all your patients, Ms. Jefferson?"

"Usually, Mr. Stevens."

He wobbled—there was no other word for it—as he hesitantly placed his feet one in front of the other.

"You're doing fine."

"Yeah, I know. Just like all the crips in those oldtime movies." The sarcasm didn't cover the pain or the self-pity. She would have to work on that.

"Nah, the crips couldn't walk. You're just blind."

He stopped. "I don't appreciate the cracks."

"No joke. Just a statement." Her voice softened. "I work with blind people, Rand. True, you've lost something very precious, but there are ways around this."

His features hardened, and she knew she'd said something wrong. "Yeah, I've lost something precious." His steps were no longer careful as he strode forward recklessly. "And my sight is a small thing in comparison. You have no idea how I feel, so don't start that psychoanalyzing garbage with me."

Elizabeth stepped in front of him to stop his reckless forward motion. But before she could warn him, he was there, running into her. His hard chest knocked her backward.

Hard arms closed around her as both fought and regained balance. She rested her hands on his bare shoulders, took a deep breath of relief and inhaled his scent.

Rand stilled. But so did she. It had been a long time since she'd been in a man's arms, and this felt so right—and wrong. She wanted to shudder, but whether at how good it felt or memories of past fears, she wasn't sure. Embarrassed, she looked toward Rand to apologize and saw his tortured look.

His hand on her lower back flexed slightly, and she knew from his expression he was remembering his wife. Her heart twisted. She smoothed her hands on his muscled shoulders and wondered how to extract herself without wounding him further. "I'm sorry, Rand. I didn't want you rushing headlong into a wall. I was going to warn you I'd stepped in front of you, but you were just too fast."

Her words broke the spell. Rand dropped his arms and

allowed her to move back. "Look, I know you don't care to go downstairs—"

"You got that right, lady. The only reason I'm doing it is to get you out of my room. I'm sure you're going to be sorry you ever suggested it."

"There need to be a few ground rules. We go together the first few times, until you know your way around without help. I don't want you to feel uncomfortable in your own house. That's why I'm here, to teach you how to be at ease. It's really very simple, once you catch on. But no more rushing around until you know your house."

"I've lived here years."

She heard the bleak note in his voice and decided it was time for another joke.

"Hey, what did the chicken say when he crossed the road?"

Rand's attention turned from his feelings to her. "What did he *say?*"

"Cluck-a cluck-a cluck-a *squaaaaawk!*"

She burst out laughing, but when he didn't even emit a chuckle her laughter died. She sighed, as if totally exasperated. "You see, a chicken clucks until it's hit. Then it hollers, as in squawk."

He grimaced, and she was elated at even that small reaction, but she didn't tell him so. She continued with her explanation. "I *love* that joke. It's one of my favorites." Not giving him a chance to comment, she turned toward the door. "Come on. I want you to take my elbow, sorta like we're out on a date or something, and we'll go downstairs together. That way, you have control. I'm not leading you."

She started out slowly across the main room of his suite, counting each step low, as if for her own benefit, although she'd already memorized how many steps to each door. "Couch on the left and TV on opposite wall. Table at sixteen steps." She paused and turned toward the left. "Door, one, two three..."

"Do you always tell such awful jokes?" he asked when she paused in the hallway. He dropped his hand from her elbow.

She was surprised he asked. "I like them. I guess jokes are in the eye of the beholder."

When he touched her elbow, she started ahead. "You want to hear another?"

"No, thank you."

She grinned. When they reached the stairway she paused. "How many steps down?"

He opened his mouth to answer, then paused, surprise on his face. "I don't know."

"Ha! Don't know your house as good as you thought, do you, Mr. Stevens? Count them on the way down."

He scowled. But when he started to take his first step his scowl was replaced by fear. She watched his left hand grip the banister while his right hand bit into her elbow. She wished the banister on the other side of the stairway was close enough for her to reach. She was afraid if he tripped she wouldn't be able to hold him. And she didn't want Max, who was peeking out of a room across the way, to see her lose control of her patient the first day. That's all she needed, for Rand to fall. Of course she knew he wouldn't be injured. She would be able to block him, but she would be black and blue for weeks, and probably out of a job. And for some reason, since the moment she had seen Rand sitting in tangled sheets on the bed, she had been drawn to him, unlike her other patients. The look on his face—she knew she could get rid of that despair if she was just given a chance. Why it was so important, more important than other cases similar to this one, she wasn't sure. It just was. Rand Stevens had gone right to her heart, pulling her heart strings, begging for something—what, she wasn't sure. But she would help him—*if* she didn't fall flat on her face right now, that is.

Fortunately, they made it down without any mishap. "Twenty-four steps."

"That's right. Now we'll continue on to the breakfast room. It's smaller and I'd prefer to eat in there."

She heard his breathing slow and knew he had finally caught his breath. "You ready?"

"Do I have a choice?"

"No."

They started across the room. She could tell Rand was nervous. He'd become belligerent again. She suspected it was because he was coming to realize that life was going to go on. As soon as he accepted that, he would again be willing to learn and not fight her. But until then, she would have to put up with his moodiness.

"Taking an awful chance coming down here with me, weren't you, Ms. Jefferson?"

"Call me Elizabeth."

"What if I'd fallen? I could have hurt you. What would you have done if I'd knocked you down the stairs and broken your back? Hmm...you could have been paralyzed."

"Like science fiction, do you?"

"I don't read it. But it doesn't do any good to change the subject—"

"I just thought maybe you did, listening to you talk." She laughed. "Really, Mr. Stevens, what you are suggesting is very unlikely."

His frown intensified, but before he could comment

his stomach growled. She paused when she heard it, and he flushed. "I told you I was hungry," was all he said.

"Evidently not hungry enough to eat your first tray," she replied.

She pushed open the door to the breakfast room and they entered. Stopping in the brightly lit room by the dark wood table she explained how his plate was set up, the placing of the silverware and anything else he might need to know about the meal.

"Any questions?"

"Yeah. Maybe I should nickname you Attila the Hun. Do you organize everyone's food this way? Or do you just take a perverse pleasure in having complete control over me?"

"Perverse pleasure," she said with relish then added, "Actually, I'm trying to give you control. If your meals are always prepared in the same way you'll know where to find your food and won't have to struggle. It's the little things that are going to make the difference, Mr. Stevens."

"You called me Rand earlier," he muttered, reaching for his ham sandwich.

"But you insist on calling me Ms. Jefferson, and I let you set the tone of our relationship."

"Relationship?" He paused with his fingers around the sandwich, an eyebrow raised in what she would have called amusement if he hadn't been upset with her.

She flushed. "You know what I mean."

"Do I?"

Oh, boy. She'd given him a chink in her armor, and he was going to use it.

"Of course. Patient-therapist relationship."

"Uh-huh. Whatever you say."

He bit into his sandwich, and she could have sworn

he smiled with pleasure—either for getting the best of her or the sandwich, she wasn't sure. She was going to believe it was because of the sandwich. After all, he hadn't had breakfast. And as she watched, he ate four bites of his sandwich before setting it down, so he evidently was very hungry. She was pleased with his progress. Until the not-so-unthinkable happened.

He tipped his glass over.

Oh, no, she thought.

His features hardened. "Try to train a crip and see what happens? I spill my milk like a two-year-old."

"It's okay—"

But she got no further. With one sweep of his hand he sent the plate and glass flying. Grabbing for the napkin in his lap, he instead caught the edge of the tablecloth, and the vase of fresh daisies and roses went tumbling. A low curse slipped from between his thinned lips. He pushed his chair back, sending it toppling, and with hands outstretched started for the door.

"Wait. Rand!"

Elizabeth jumped up and headed after him. Evidently, Rand did know his house somewhat. He made it all the way to the stairs before stumbling. Another curse slipped past his lips.

"What's going on here? What happened?" Max came rushing out of his den.

"Get her out of here!" Rand demanded, doing his best to get to his feet. He grabbed the banister and started climbing the stairs.

"Stay out of this," Elizabeth warned Max, sprinting after her patient. "Listen to me, Rand. It was an accident. You didn't expect to be perfect the first day, did you?"

"Get away from me, lady. I don't want you anywhere near me."

"Forget it, I'm your nurse."

Reaching the top of the stairs, he turned and headed toward his room, knocking over a hallway table in the process. "I don't want you."

"Good. Fine. But I'm still here. I've got a job to do, and indulging in self-pity isn't going to help your cause."

"Self-pity!" He waved his arms wildly as he crossed his room, feeling for anything to show him where he was. So much for counting.

She followed him into his room and watched as he lunged toward the bed. His knees hit it, then his hands, as he patted, getting his bearings. Finally, secure in his position, he turned to face her, opening his mouth to blast her again. But she beat him to the punch.

"Well, self-pity or injured pride. I'll give you the choice. Which is it?"

Suddenly, he sniffed. Tilting his head, he turned it slightly as if he could see his room. Then his face snapped toward hers. "Someone's been in here and cleaned my room. You had someone clean my room, didn't you!"

Chapter Three

"Well, of course I did," she said, as if it was the most natural thing in the world. "I guess it's the fresh lemony smell that gave it away, huh? Or maybe finding the floor clear of clutter as you raced across it?"

Rand wanted to choke her. But he knew he wouldn't be able to find her throat if he struck out. He could tell she was near the door, out of his reach.

Realizing his train of thought, he was horrified. He had never struck a woman in his life and here he was contemplating strangulation. Still, he felt totally out of control, a feeling that had plagued him since that night just over a year ago... Today he'd felt a few minutes of relief when he'd gone downstairs and been able to sit at the table, eating a sandwich. Now the control was gone again. "You said you wouldn't clean my room."

"*Au contraire,* Mr. Stevens. I didn't say I wouldn't clean it. I said you could have my company while I cleaned your room or while we had lunch."

Anger spiraled through him. Anger, and a spark of admiration. Not one of the nurses who had been hired since he'd come home had stood up so well, or come back with such snappy answers. If he wasn't so furious, he might smile. But he *was* angry, so he *wasn't* going to smile. "How am I supposed to find my things since you rearranged everything?"

She had the audacity to snort. "Just what did you want?"

He paused. He certainly couldn't tell her that he didn't want anything. So he said the first thing that came to his mind. "I wanted my blue pants. They were near the end of the bed." Or at least, since he had thrown most of the clothes down there that Max had tried to dress him in, he ventured that's where they'd been.

He heard her walk to the closest and rummage around. "Here you go." A pair of pants was thrust into his hands. "What else?"

A perverse stubborn streak swept through him. "My white shirt. The one with the satiny white stripes through it."

He heard some more rummaging. "We'll have to get this closet in order so you can find your clothes your-self."

He wanted to grin. It was the first time he had been in control with this woman, and he was enjoying it. She came toward him and thrust the soft shirt into his hands. He caught a faint smell of her citrus perfume, light, airy, reminding him of sunshine.

"Anything else?"

It was said so sweetly, but he wasn't fooled. She wouldn't like waiting on him like a maid. She was a professional, someone sent to train him, not perform me-nial duties for him. "Yeah, I'd like a pair of oxford socks."

He heard her digging around, and then they were

placed in his hand. "Anything else? How about I draw your bath?"

She was goading him. And since he couldn't think of another thing for her to pull out of his dresser he decided to take his anger out in a way she wouldn't be able to challenge with that sweet voice of hers. "I need help dressing."

Dead silence followed. All he could hear was the small breaths she took. They sounded a little rapid. Had he finally shocked her? A satisfied smile curved his mouth.

But when soft hands suddenly touched his bare arms it was he who was surprised. "What are you doing?" he questioned as she took the clothes from him.

"Helping you to dress. Now, really, the easiest way to get a shirt on is to button it from bottom to top." She was slipping it on his arms. First the left, then the right. He tried to follow the sound of her voice by turning his head, but she was too quick. This woman was expeditious in everything she did.

"I can—"

"Like this," she interrupted and began on his buttons. Her small warm hands slipped one button at a time in their slots, working their way up his shirt, gently brushing his skin as she went. It had been so long since he'd held a woman. Over a year. Since his wife had died. He'd thought all feeling died with her, but these tiny hands, that fragrant scent, the husky voice... He found himself reacting to her!

He would have collapsed, he was so shocked, had she not continued talking.

"Now for your pants—"

"I think I can manage," he choked out, embarrassed. She was his therapist. He was blind. He wasn't supposed to notice things like how tall she was, or how fragile her hands felt as they touched him, or how small her elbow was. His thoughts shook him to the marrow of his bones. He jerked his pants from her. "If you don't mind," he replied acidly, doing his best to deny his emotions, "I can dress myself. I have no further need of you."

There was a pause, then Elizabeth's voice came back, some hint of emotion in it that he couldn't identify. "I'm sure you don't. I'll be back in half an hour to discuss your closets and the placing of your clothes." He heard her move toward the door. "And Mr. Stevens?"

He didn't want to answer, he only wanted her gone. But he knew she wouldn't leave until he acknowledged her. "Yes?"

"We'll have dinner at five-thirty."

"Foul woman," he muttered, sinking onto the edge of the bed. He immediately lunged up and felt his way to the door. Sixteen steps, she'd said. Sure enough, the door was right where it should be. He pushed it closed. He was never certain that someone wasn't standing there watching him. He hated not knowing.

Going back to the bed, he shed his pajama bottoms so he could pull on his pants. He could certainly dress himself without someone hovering over him. Rand had been used to being in control. He'd had thousands of employees who had depended on him every day, a wife who had relied on him—at least until the accident.

Grief welled in him, though not as sharp as a year ago, but still there just the same. His wife was dead. He took only a little comfort in the fact that she was in heaven. He still missed her. It was because of him that she'd been taken before her time. She'd wanted children, wanted to be a mother, and he'd robbed her of all that in one disastrous accident. They'd had their entire life planned out. Everything was going their way. They had decided to wait until Carolyn had finished college and they had spent some time together to get to know one another before they'd have children. They had wanted two, with two and a half years between their births so they would still be young when the children were grown. After the children grew up they'd planned to make sure each child had part of the land this house sat on. One thousand acres of prime land he and his wife had invested in to make sure their children's future would be financially secure. They also wanted that much so they wouldn't have close neighbors. They'd planned to slowly build it up. They'd put in a pool last year. They'd even started college funds for the two children they planned to have. Everything was under control, all was ready for them to start their family. The auto accident had destroyed everything.

His wife was dead, their plans in the dust, and he had no control over anything he did. It was a terrifying feeling. He should have been more careful driving. Carolyn had told him of the thunderstorm warning and suggested they put off going to the party until the rain let up. He was a good driver. He hadn't worried. And it had cost his wife her life.

Sighing, Rand stood and pulled his pants on, then zipped them. He folded the sleeves of his white shirt to his elbows. He felt for his socks, then headed for the door, but paused. How long had it been since he'd been out of this room? The only time he'd left his bed was when he'd first got home and Max had forced him into the other room to listen to the TV or stereo.

But Max had stopped insisting when Rand refused to cooperate. And, at the time, Rand had thought that was what he wanted. He didn't like being bothered, wanted

to be left alone. As long as he was in his room, in his
bed, nothing could go wrong.

But it had. He'd become bitter, lashing out at everyone and everything that got in his way, even Max, he
suddenly realized. He'd allowed his fear and bitterness
to fester, eat away at him, until he was certain there was
nothing left but a shell.

He hated what he had become, but it was safe, too.
When his wife had died he'd been devastated. He refused to turn to anyone, including God, for comfort. On
some deep level he felt he deserved what had happened
to him as penance for his wife's death. Oh, he knew
how foolish that was, yet the feeling was there. He
couldn't explain it to anyone so he'd simply withdrawn,
keeping a protective shield about him. His room was his.
No one would come in and invade his shield.

Until this newest therapist. Elizabeth hadn't batted an
eyelid about coming into his room and rearranging it the
way she wanted it. She'd had the audacity to sit in front
of him and eat his breakfast, making him feel like a two-
year-old throwing a temper tantrum.

Then she'd narrowed in on his weakness. By threat-
ening his room, she'd known he would have to go downstairs just to show her he could fight back. And now,
standing before this threshold he'd crossed very rarely
since coming home, he suspected he'd been maneuvered
into dressing, too. Elizabeth Jefferson was entirely too
perceptive for his own good. He'd have to do something
about that. And he had an idea.

He had found a weak spot in the soft-spoken, sweet-
smelling Ms. Jefferson.

She was attracted to him, too. He had to admit there
was something elemental about her that drew him. He
wasn't sure what. He knew it wasn't her looks—he

couldn't see her. Her smell was very attractive—the sweet citrus scent she wore drove him to distraction—but it was more. There was life in her. That's what he sensed, a vitality that brought light, so to speak, into the room she was in. He wasn't sure why, but it was there, drawing him. Considering it had been a year since his wife's death and a year since he'd even thought of a woman, he was totally floored by his feelings. He'd been given a special wife, one he'd planned to love to his dying day. He wasn't interested in replacing her, ever, and suddenly here was this woman, awaking emotions he'd thought never to feel again.

But that wouldn't stop him from using her attraction to repel her. When he'd held her in his arms he'd felt her reaction, the quickened breathing, the tentative exploration of her fingers on his shoulders. Had she known he was thinking of his wife and wondering how he could be attracted to another woman? Or had she been too caught up in her realization of him as a man?

He smiled. She hadn't liked that she'd seen him as more than a patient.

Feeling his face, he realized he needed to shave. His hair needed brushing, too. Rand knew he wasn't ready for the changes Elizabeth Jefferson was attempting to bring about in his life. He had lived this past year isolated and alone and he would be happy to stay that way for a while longer.

Are you sure? a tiny voice whispered, reminding him of his loneliness and the close relationship he missed with his brother.

"I'm sure," he muttered, thinking that loneliness was a small price to pay for the knowledge that he'd be safe in his solitude. Safe from any more accidents or losses. Safe from the world.

* * *

"Are you sure this is working out like you were planning?"

Elizabeth was sitting in Max's den, staring across the desk at her employer. She'd come down knowing he'd want to talk to her and figuring if there were going to be fireworks, they might as well be out of earshot of Rand.

"Well, not exactly. He's actually more advanced than most patients I've worked with."

Max shook his head, then smiled. "I'd hate to see some of your other patients."

"I'm sure you would."

"You really think he's making progress?"

"I didn't say that. I said he is further along than most of my patients. I think he's ready to forge ahead. Actually, I think he wouldn't mind having some control over his life again, as long as it's not too much. Tell me, has he said anything to you about the accident?"

Max shook his head. "Nothing. Just that he doesn't want to talk about it."

She nodded, expecting as much. "I don't want you to be discouraged by what you saw today—"

"Actually, I feel just the opposite. I couldn't believe my brother actually came down to lunch. However, when I came out of my office, I was afraid Rand was going to hurt you."

She laughed. "Rand would never hurt me."

Max lifted an eyebrow. Realizing what she had said, she blushed. "Your brother is frustrated, angry and frightened. He's not going to strike out at me physically. I think he's just about exhausted that avenue."

"What do you mean?"

"Well, while he was in bed and refused to get up that

might have been a possibility. After all, how many ways are there to take frustrations out? But he's up and moving around now. And your brother is smart. He's probably figured out that temper tantrums aren't going to scare me away. He'll think up something else.''

''You make my brother sound calculating.''

She sobered. ''Not at all. He's scared, and this is his way of fighting it. I noticed earlier a pool outside. Does Rand know how to swim?''

''Why, yes, he does. It's one of—was one of his favorite pastimes.''

''I noticed he had trouble breathing after coming down the stairs. I would like to work on getting him to exercise. If he likes swimming, then maybe I'll get him into the pool.''

''But what about—won't, um—''

Elizabeth leaned forward. ''He'll be fine. I'll be there with him. He needs some way to expend his energy. I think this will be very beneficial. I'll also need to run into town tomorrow. There are some things I'd like to pick up for him.''

''I'd like to go with you, if you don't mind.''

Surprised, Elizabeth nodded.

''I want to see what you do, be involved somehow in Rand's healing.''

She smiled. ''I understand.'' Looking at him, she asked something she'd always wondered about. ''Being a twin, what's it like?''

Max sighed. ''The best and worst can be applied to being a twin. You always have a playmate, someone to confide in. But in a twin's case, or at least our case, there was no lying to each other. There were emotions between us stronger than between the average siblings so we always knew what the other one was feeling.

"And then there was growing up. People used to call us by both of our names when they weren't sure who was who. We hated it when we were dressed the same for pictures. But then again, there was an upside. We could dress the same and fool friends."

Max suddenly smiled. "I remember one incident. Rand got mad at me when I wouldn't listen to him about this girl. So, since he thought I was being stubborn, he went over to my girlfriend's house and confessed to her, acting as me, of course, that I had been dating another girl—*several* other girls in fact—behind her back and now I wasn't sure who to ask to the senior prom."

"He didn't," Elizabeth said, laughing, trying to imagine the scene. "What did you do?"

"Well, Trish wouldn't speak to me and I couldn't figure out why until, in a spurt of guilt, Rand confessed. I think that's one of the few times we've come to blows. And Mom came in and read us the riot act for fighting in the house, then sent us outside to finish it."

"Did you?"

Max smiled. "Nah. Mom's intervention took the focus off each other long enough that we cooled down. We then discussed it and worked it out. I went to Trish and explained. She was furious with my brother and said some really nasty things, and I broke up with her. I found out that she wasn't as important as I thought, and that Rand was right, she was out just to date a twin—an oddity."

"I suppose that special empathy is why you have circles under your eyes right now?" Elizabeth asked gently.

"I am pretty worried about him. I don't know of anyone I care more for."

"You know that everything's going to work out for the best."

Max cocked his head. "Can I ask you a question?"

Put on guard, afraid he might have discovered something of her past, Elizabeth carefully answered with a small laugh. "Sure. I don't know if I'll answer, though."

"Are you... Do you go to church?"

Relief flooded her. "Yes, I do."

"I wondered. Too many things you've said have sounded like some of the memory verses I've learned in the past."

Elation filled her. "And Rand?"

Max's smile faded. "He was pretty strong in church until the accident. He's so distant now. I sometimes think he blames God for what happened."

"It wouldn't be too uncommon. Your brother has suffered a terrible loss. Even if he doesn't blame God, exactly, he might know that by continuing a close walk with God he'd have to forgive himself."

Max's eyes widened. "You think he is purposely holding himself apart from God as a way of punishment?"

"I don't know. Have the doctors told you they think Rand's symptoms might be psychosomatic?"

Max frowned. "I don't believe that."

"I'm not saying it's true. I'm just saying that maybe they sense guilt pricking him and that's where they got the idea that he might be causing his blindness. If that's so, then I would think maybe that's why he's running from God instead of actually blaming him."

Max sat back, an amazed expression crossing his face. "Do you give all of your patients advice like this?"

She blushed and lowered her eyes. "No. I just, well, I've been thinking about Rand since you came to my office. I was afraid something was not quite right in his life besides the blindness. From the way you'd described him to me it seemed like he'd lost more than his wife, like maybe he'd lost his faith. You made it sound like he'd given up on everything. And since you seemed to be so in touch with his feelings I tended toward the belief that you were right in what you said. Despite the fact that some relatives overreact. Anyway,'' she continued, ''it helps to have my suspicions confirmed.''

"So, what do we do? He refuses to go to church or even talk about happier times with me."

"All we can do is wait and allow God to work His miracles," she said, knowing that meant more than just sitting around, but taking every opportunity that was open to her to help Rand discover life again.

Max shook his head and a small rueful smile curved his lips. "I'm glad you're Rand's therapist, not mine. You'd run me in circles with all of this—just like I have a feeling you're going to do to Rand."

"I'm not a miracle worker," she warned, afraid of the sound in his voice.

"No. But at least you know who is."

She shook her head, then stood. "If you want, you can join us for supper tonight. I don't want Rand to think I'm isolating him."

"But isn't that what you're doing?"

Elizabeth grinned. "Not exactly. I need him to trust me, but he needs you there, too."

"Fine. I plan on going into the office the rest of the afternoon. I think it's time I started going in at least half of each day, and maybe a full day since you're here now—that is, if you're still planning on sticking around."

"Well, as I told Rand, I'll be here for at least a month since I spent part of the advance." She winked.

He laughed. "Rand's not going to be able to resist you."

She walked to the door. "See you at supper." But as she left, she wondered if maybe the proper question should not be if Rand was going to be able to resist her, but if she was going to be able to resist Rand?

Chapter Four

"Which side of a chicken has the most feathers?"

Rand sighed loud and long. Well, that was an improvement, Elizabeth thought.

"No guess?"

He crossed his arms and turned his face toward the window. "I don't like jokes," he growled.

A definite improvement, she amended. He was answering questions. "Okay. I'll tell you. The outside."

When he said nothing, she explained. "You see, most people are thinking right side or left, so they never even think about—"

"A joke isn't funny if you have to explain it."

She laughed and came into the room. Rand was sitting on the sofa in the main part of his suite. The drapes were open—she'd told the maid to make sure to open his drapes even though he was blind—and he was turned so the sunlight was striking one side of his face as he absorbed its heat. He looked much better than this morning, though he did need to shave. Dark stubble showed it had been at least three days since he'd shaved. Max had said he refused to shave and only allowed someone to shave him when his beard got long. Well, she'd take care of that soon. She was thoroughly excited with the progress he had made in only one day. He had certainly been ready for someone to step in and bully him back to the living again.

"You know, Rand, I don't think you'd know funny if it jumped out and bit you."

He sighed again. "I just enjoy a good joke."

"Oh, yeah? Name one."

He opened his mouth, paused, then closed it. "You're not going to get me to participate in this ridiculous game of one-upmanship when it comes to jokes."

"Oh, well, it was worth a try. I've about run out of chicken jokes."

"Does this mean I won't have to hear any more?" he asked hopefully.

"Actually, it means that out of all of my patients I've had, and friends, for that matter, I have just about used up the jokes I know, not that *you've* heard them all. So, are you ready to go to dinner?"

"Do I have a choice?"

"Yes. But if you decide to stay, I get to tell you all the funny parts of my favorite movies."

He stood. She saw his hesitancy and walked forward. Turning, she inched her elbow back, allowing him to feel it as it brushed his arm. "Max will be joining us tonight."

"I don't want to go down."

She paused. She'd been afraid of this. "He's your brother."

"Actually, I'm not feeling good at all." He sat down. "I'm certain I'm catching the flu."

She grinned. So, he was going back to his old games. "Do you really expect me to believe that, Mr. Stevens?"

"I don't care what you believe," he said. "You're only my therapist, not my mother."

She watched him lie on the couch and close his eyes. "Go on. Leave me alone."

Surly. That was a good word to describe his tone. So how was she going to get him to move? She grinned. "You sure you're sick?"

She saw the muscles of his face relax with relief. "Yes. I'm feeling very ill. I really didn't want to go down, but I decided to humor you. But I refuse to expose my brother to whatever virus I am coming down with."

She rolled her eyes.

"Now will you leave me alone?"

"Okay," she said with great reluctance. Letting him believe he'd won, she went into the hall. Now what?

A slow smile spread across her face as an idea came to her. She crossed to her room, went into the bathroom and gathered up everything she thought she'd need. She went back to his room. He had already risen and gone to his bed. For someone not feeling good, he was quick.

Hearing a sound, Rand raised his head slightly. "Who's there?" He paused. "What are you doing back?" He'd obviously smelled her perfume, since her walk couldn't be heard on the carpet...unless he had really good hearing.

"You said you were sick."

"And I told you to leave."

"Impossible."

"I'm not kidding."

"Neither am I. What would your brother think if I deserted you when you weren't feeling good?"

She set a bowl full of water and alcohol on the bedside

table then eased herself onto the bed next to him, her hip touching his.

"What do you think you're doing? What's that smell? Alcohol?"

"Good senses." She squeezed out a washcloth and slapped it against his forehead. "This will help a headache or fever, or so I've heard."

"What in the—"

She pulled a thermometer out of her shirt pocket and jammed it into his mouth. "Now let's see what type of temperature you have."

"Lady, you're demented," he muttered around the thermometer, waving his hands in the air. She leaned back to keep from getting slapped. In one sweep, the washcloth was knocked aside, then her hands were captured. "I don't want your help. I don't want everyone staring at me. I'm happy here, in my room, alone."

For emphasis, he shook her wrists, jerking her forward. Losing her balance, she ended up half across Rand. "I know."

He stilled. His fingers flexed on her wrists, gentling. He leaned his head forward and inhaled close to her neck. But he didn't say anything.

"Don't you understand I can't let you do that?"

"What?" he asked, his voice low, vibrating through his chest, sending sparks of awareness through her.

"I can't let you hide up here. You've been allowed to be alone too long. Your brother's heart is breaking. He misses you."

Any other argument might not have worked, but Elizabeth remembered what Max had said about that special bond between them. Rand had to know Max was hurting.

Finally, Rand whispered, "I can't go down there and make a mess again."

"You won't."

"How can you be so sure?"

"You're an achiever, Rand. You can do whatever you put your mind to. But let me tell you something else. This is your brother we're talking about, the same one who about beat you when you told Trish he had other girls."

"How do you know about that?"

She grinned. "He told me. Do you think someone that would risk your ire to prove something like that would care if you spilled a glass of milk as you're relearning everything?"

Before he could answer, a throat was cleared. Elizabeth's eyes flew to the door. Max, looking very forbidding, was standing there. "Are you ready to go?" he asked, and there was a note of disapproval in his voice.

She swallowed. Pushing away, for Rand had immediately released her wrists when he'd heard his brother, she eyed Rand. "We were just having a discussion. But I think we're ready. Aren't we, Rand?"

She was afraid he was going to say no. There was nothing more she could do. Instead, he nodded curtly. Elizabeth stood. Rand swung his feet around and followed suit. Then, reaching out, he took Elizabeth's elbow and started across the room with her. Max raised an eyebrow but said nothing. He turned and went into the hallway.

Supper was served in the breakfast room. They had soup followed by hot roast beef sandwiches. She figured since she was asking so much it would be easier to serve simple foods that he would have little trouble eating. Later, as he got used to coming down, they would increase their fare to harder meals to deal with. She allowed Rand to seat himself then went to her chair. Max pulled it out, which Rand noted. Then Max seated himself.

"So, how was your day at the office, Max?"

Startled at first he glanced from Elizabeth to Rand. At her encouraging nod, he sighed. "Jennifer is going to drive me crazy."

"Who's she?" Elizabeth asked, picking up her spoon and starting her soup. Rand was ill at ease, his spoon shaking as he dragged it across the edge of his bowl attempting to get some soup. She didn't comment. Let him think no one was paying attention to him.

"Rand's secretary." There was an awkward pause. "I mean, she was—is…" He sighed. "I'm doing that part now, for awhile. Anyway, she burst into tears again today and disappeared for an hour. I was left with another secretary who scolded me severely, saying I was much too hard on Jennifer." Max set his spoon down. "I told her to send a memo to the head buyer of women's accessories informing her to get rid of the cheaper jewelry I've seen out on the counter. However, she got that mixed up with the order to increase the fall sweater stock by ten percent that was going to the men's department. Needless to say, I got a call from the person in charge of the men's department insisting I was making a horrible mistake. But it was only *after* the orders had been filled and all the costume jewelry had been bought that someone contacted me. I will admit, I was a little angry. But the girl is so sensitive."

"She's intimidated by you."

Both heads swung in Rand's direction. Max's face lit with hope. Elizabeth wanted to ask if he'd ever aired problems in front of Rand before, but could tell by his face that he hadn't. He was realizing this might have been a way to reach Rand. "What do you mean? I don't intimidate people."

"She's had a crush on you since she came to work for the company. You probably make her nervous. If you'd bring her in, talk to her, joke a bit, you'd probably solve the problem."

Max looked astonished. "A crush? But she's only eighteen, nineteen years old."

Rand grinned a long-suffering grin. "Exactly."

"Did she have a crush on you—"

"No. Always you, brother."

"Well, okay. Fine. I'll talk to her. I can't believe... But that still does me no good with the jewelry. I've got buckets of the stuff and no way to get rid of it."

"Attach it to the sweaters and dresses in the women's department. Mark up the outfits a small price to cover the jewelry, then promote it as a seasonal special."

"Good idea. But how—"

"Mary will know what to do. She's handled situations like that before."

"So that's why you keep her over women's. She's driven me crazy sending memos on things needing to be done. I haven't known what to tell her. I guess I'm just too used to handling the financial end of things and not dealing with the actual working end, the people end."

Rand shrugged and started on his sandwich. Elizabeth noticed almost all of his soup was gone. Good. Get his mind off his disability and it was easier for him to function. She wondered again if he had figured out he was going to go on living and was ready to take that step.

A silence descended and everyone ate. Rand was careful as he reached for his cup, sliding his hand forward slowly, feeling everything until his fingers brushed his teacup. He sipped then slid the cup back to where it had been. Max witnessed this and fidgeted. Elizabeth knew he'd get used to it, eventually.

Max interrupted her thoughts with a nervous clearing of his throat. "So, what time do you want to go into town tomorrow, Elizabeth?"

"Around nine okay?"

"You're going to town?" Frowning, Rand stopped eating his sandwich.

"As a matter of fact, yes. Max offered to take me since he had some errands to run, too."

Rand's mouth twisted sardonically. "I'm sure he did. I thought you said we were going to work on my rehabilitation."

Max raised surprised eyebrows. Elizabeth wasn't sure what to think. "Well, we are. I have a few things I need to pick up along that line."

"With Max?"

Max leaned back in his chair and grinned. She shot a curious look between them, feeling as if she was the butt of a joke. So, as was her style, she took the offensive. "Of course. You see, I'll need his expertise."

Max frowned and she noted with a small grin that his frown was almost identical to the one Rand now wore. "What expertise is that?" Rand asked.

"Why, I need his help since I need to buy you some bathing trunks. You see, Rand, tomorrow you're going to go swimming."

Chapter Five

"I don't like this," Rand said, and it was obvious from the way his hands fidgeted near his trunks that he didn't. Rand had been next to impossible to get into the trunks, and now he stood outside the dressing room door near the pool looking mutinous.

Feeling just a little mutinous herself, Elizabeth said, "Why'd the chicken cross the road?"

"I don't want to hear another joke." He scowled.

Elizabeth smiled and came forward. Flicking her finger against the waistband of his trunks, she whispered, "To keep from getting plucked."

Rand's mouth fell open. She sauntered out of reach.

"Are you implying you plucked me by making me dress in these ridiculous trunks?"

They certainly didn't look ridiculous to her. As a matter of fact, Rand was devastating to Elizabeth's senses. His large muscular body still looked good in a set of blue and red trunks despite the months of missed workouts. She was embarrassed to admit that, though, so she'd told her joke, trying to knock him down a peg. It hadn't worked. He still looked sexy and just as manly as he had a minute ago.

Still, she only said, "You want to fight with me you better learn how to do it right. Besides, why do you feel ridiculous? You look great." She hoped there hadn't been a note of wistful longing in her voice.

If there had, Rand was too upset to notice. "I know what I look like but I feel isolated here. Like everyone's looking at me and I can't look back."

Uh-oh…she knew where he was going with this. And in a way, he was right. "To put you more at ease, I have on a black suit. It dips slightly in the front and has two hot pink and neon blue strips going from the right shoulder to the left hip. Thin straps. And the suit plunges low in the back."

A speculative gleam crossed his face. "Blue and pink. Can I trace them?"

She flushed, knowing he was trying to embarrass her and succeeding. "In your dreams, pal."

He scowled.

"Come on. You've distracted me enough. Let's get into the pool."

"I've distracted you, have I?"

"Not *that* way," she warned. His warm hand touched her elbow and shivers passed through her body. Rand was too handsome for his own good. She glided across the green indoor-outdoor carpet until she got to the edge of the pool. "Remember, three steps here. The water might throw your balance off a bit."

"I've swum all my life," he growled.

Elizabeth glanced at the glass enclosure, the well-tended tropical trees and expensive-looking poolside furniture and had to wonder if he had always been swimming in such luxury. She didn't ask. As soon as Rand's feet touched the water, he gratefully sank into its depths. Before she could say anything he dived and swam off.

"Wait!"

But it was too late. She swam after him, keeping just out of his reach, and it didn't take long for him to realize his mistake. Surfacing, he reached around, panicked.

"You started at an angle. Go to your left about three feet and you'll find the side."

He stroked over and then latched onto the side. Fear was slowly replaced by frustration.

She didn't say anything, only treaded water a few feet away, waiting.

Finally, he whispered, "I forgot I couldn't see. The water, it brought back memories and I simply swam, thinking of the freedom that comes when I swim. Then I started to do some laps but suddenly didn't know where I was."

"You'll learn."

"I don't *want* to learn. I've been swimming my entire life. I thought with this, at least..." His voice trailed off.

Elizabeth swam forward until she was right in front of him where her feet could touch the ground. "This will be one of the easy things to learn—honest," she added when he opened his mouth. "I know it's hard. You're blind. Your entire world has been turned upside down. But with a little work, a little thought, you'll conquer this. I was going to warn you to find the edge of the pool, count off strokes with me swimming by you. We would measure the pool, learn it, then let you go on your own. I guess I should have explained it all to you before we got in."

"I want to do things again. It's been so long, sometimes it seems like a lifetime. But—" he paused and dropped his head, weariness etched on his face "—I've never in my life been scared until my eyesight was taken from me. I've told you more about my fears in the past two days than I've ever told anyone in my entire life."

She rested her hand on his arm. "Your feelings are normal."

He raised his head. "Are they?" Something changed in the air around them. Instead of seeing him as her patient, or even her student, she suddenly recognized him as a man, and she wondered if he was thinking of her as a woman. When his grip tightened and he pulled her forward, she was certain. "Rand, I don't think—"

"Good. Don't think," he whispered. "I've been wanting to do this since you first walked into my room."

Wrapping his arm around her waist, Rand pulled her forward and with his hand, traced her face. Finding her lips, he ran his thumb over them before finally lowering his mouth to hers. Soft, gentle insistence met Elizabeth's reluctant embrace, causing her to melt. He tasted, nibbling at her lower lip until she let him increase the intimacy of the kiss, and then he was pulling back, easing room between them. His left hand traced her face, looking at her in his own way, following her high cheekbones, her eyes, brushing her eyelashes before touching her nose. Finally his hand cupped her cheek. "You're beautiful. I only wish I could see—"

"But you did," she whispered, stepping back. "I would have taught you that eventually, but evidently you were ready to learn how to use your hands."

She was still backing up.

"Don't run from me, Elizabeth."

That was the first time he'd used her name, and it sent shivers of longing down her spine. It sounded so good on his lips. "I'm not running. I just don't think what happened is a good idea."

"Why not?"

"Well, because you need to keep your mind on learning right now. I'm a therapist, not a girlfriend."

"Girlfriend? Now there's a term I haven't heard in the last fifteen years. I'm thirty-two years old. Girlfriend sounds so teenagerish, like something Jennifer would think of."

"Well, maybe that's why I used it."

Rand's smile left his face. "I hope you're not suggesting what I feel for you is infatuation."

"That's exactly what I'm saying."

"Well, you're wrong. All I feel for you is an attraction. I haven't known you long enough to know anything beyond that."

Elizabeth flushed. She'd had to fight off patients before, but she'd never felt anything. And to have him so bluntly state the truth pricked her pride. She tried to recover her equilibrium. "Good. In that case, I would suggest you put the attraction out of your mind so we can get on with work."

"And will you put the attraction out of your mind?"

Surely he couldn't know? "I don't know what you're talking about."

He took a few steps forward, and she matched him with steps back. "Is it Max you are attracted to? After all, his body isn't scarred and he has his sight."

She gasped.

He took that for an affirmative. "So that's why you went into town with him today. You'll work with me, but you're interested in the better brother—the one who isn't damaged goods."

"That's not true," she whispered. "This is a job to me. I won't allow my feelings to become involved with any patient—or family member. I'm getting paid to help you learn to work in your environment, nothing else."

"Yeah, sure," he muttered and headed toward the edge of the pool. "Well, then, let's not waste your time. Tell me again what we're supposed to do to count off this pool so I won't get lost. I suddenly have an intense desire to swim several laps."

Elizabeth sank onto the couch in her suite. She reached for the remote and flipped the TV to a local station. She wasn't really interested in watching the news, but she still had twenty minutes before supper. And she needed that time to gather her strength before facing Rand again.

Rand.

Now there was a dangerous man. In all of her years as a therapist she had never been the least bit interested in a patient. She couldn't believe she was now. She had allowed him to kiss her. Oh, she could dress it up and say it was him, but she'd been curious, too, and wondered what it would feel like. It had been so long since anyone had held her. She'd always told herself God's arms offered enough comfort to sustain her. And they had. For years after her devastating breakup, He'd been there at night when she'd cried out in pain, fear, loneliness, His presence a constant comfort, a reassurance. She didn't think God would ever lead anyone into her life after what had happened.

"Why, God?" she whispered. "I don't want anyone. I can't have anyone involved in my life now. It's too dangerous." Her voice dropped to a whisper. "I'm too scared."

The small quickening in her spirit spoke to her. "But I have a reason to fear," she tried to explain but knew that was a lie. God's love cast out fear. "Well, I don't *want* to care for anyone, then," she amended. "I've been fine alone."

But had she been?

Suddenly her eyes widened as she saw something familiar on the TV. Slowly straightening from her slumped position on the sofa, she watched as she and Max hurried into a local restaurant where they'd had a quick lunch after shopping for Rand. Max pulled open the door and she threw her head back and laughed. She watched herself cross the threshold with Max's hand at her waist, and the reporter's words registered. "A new love interest of corporate giant Max Stevens? Since the broken engagement two years ago Max has kept out of the limelight where his love life was concerned. However, it seems he's going public again. With his brother, Rand Stevens, who used to help run the multimillion-dollar business, now out of the picture, one has to wonder if Max is ready to settle down and start producing heirs for the family empire. Speculation has been rife since the brother's accident just what would happen to the mega kingdom if anything happened to Max—"

She flicked the TV off. Dizziness engulfed her senses, and black dots swam before her eyes. Her biggest fear about working here had just come to pass.

She stood and headed out of the room and down the stairs. She had to leave. She couldn't stay. What if Michael had seen that?

Within seconds she found herself in front of Max's study. Her knock was answered. Striding in, she stopped short when she saw Max seated in his chair, remote in his hand. He clicked the television off and without preliminaries said, "I gather you just saw what's been splashed across the network news?"

She nodded.

"Don't worry. I'm always news. The reporters hound us because of what we own. Anything Rand or I do makes the headlines. However, it'll die down in a day or two. Had I spotted the reporter, I would have called the station and asked them not to air it."

She stood in dumbfounded silence listening to him dismiss something so easily. "You could get them not to air that?" she asked, latching onto the last, unable to believe what he was saying.

He shrugged. "Money talks. We do major commercials during some of their prime time shows. It'd hurt them to lose our funds."

Slowly, the panic eased as she realized she had probably overreacted. "I don't like being a public figure."

Max stood and came around his desk, the thick carpet muffling his shoes. Taking her hands, he looked into her eyes. "I'm terribly sorry for that. About every three or four months the media decide they need to find something newsworthy to report on our business. It's especially an obsession since Rand's accident. I'll have my lawyer call the station first thing in the morning and express my displeasure at the unfounded rumors they've started. They'll back off for now. They seem to think, since I haven't dated in the last two years, that I have either not healed from a broken heart or have turned gay."

Elizabeth tried to stifle a horrified laugh. "You're kidding, right?"

He grimaced. "I only wish. I don't think today's society understands about waiting for the right one."

Any doubts Elizabeth had about this man and his brother slowly faded away. These were good people she was working for. And with those doubts, her peace was restored. She knew God had sent her here. He would make sure she was protected and that everything worked out. She was being a silly ninnyhammer, as her grandmother used to say. "I'm sorry to have panicked. I must admit that it's quite shocking to see yourself on TV when you're not expecting it. I just wish the national stations hadn't picked it up."

"Don't worry. As far as I know, it wasn't on ABC or CNN."

She laughed. "Oh, well, that's good, I suppose."

He laughed in return. "Will Rand be coming down for supper?"

"Yes. At least, when I left him in his room, he said he would. He got a good workout in the pool. I think once he relaxed and learned the basics about finding his way around in a pool, he really enjoyed it. As a matter of fact, in a week or two I'm going to be asking you to join us. I think it would go a long way to helping him heal."

Max's eyes glowed with pleasure. "I'd really like that."

"Good. Well, I'd better get up there and see if Rand is ready, or if he has decided he's mad at me again." She winked. "He's something else."

Max watched her go, a soft expression crossing his face. "Yes, Ms. Jefferson, he is," he whispered more to himself than anyone else. "But I think you haven't even discovered the half of it. And when you do, it's going to be interesting to see what you do about it." For Max knew that there was more to Rand's sudden decision to participate than met the eye. And he had an idea Elizabeth Jefferson was the main reason.

A knock on the door sounded, and Rand reluctantly called out permission to enter. He'd closed the suite's door earlier to watch TV in peace. That was when he'd heard the report about his brother and Elizabeth—and himself. They made him sound like a has-been, someone who was already dead and buried. He'd been angry that the public pictured him like that. He wasn't dead, yet. Although, thinking back over the last months, he realized he'd given every indication of being so. He'd hidden himself away, refusing to face reality. However, look how reality was, if the news was true. Elizabeth Jefferson was seen out on the town with his brother. She could give him therapy, but was interested in Max. How ironic, he thought, since she was the first person to spark something in him since his wife.

He smelled her perfume first.

"Why'd the chicken cross the road?"

The sweet, slightly husky voice drifted across the room as she approached.

"Not another one of those jokes?" he grumbled, though he was tempted to smile. He'd never met anyone who took such delight in telling such awful jokes.

"Wrong."

She was standing next to him. He tilted his head toward her and waited.

"Because it was there!"

Her laughter reminded him of tinkling bells, sweet, melodic, soothing. Maybe that's what had first attracted him, her soothing voice, not to mention her audacity to laugh despite the circumstances. Taking his tray from him, indeed, he thought, a small smile touching his lips.

"I see you liked that one, Rand."

"No." He shook his head. "I was just thinking that if they got any worse—"

"Does that mean," she interrupted with mock hurt, "that you don't want to hear my chicken jokes?"

"Yes!" he said, though he knew that wasn't true. He was starting to enjoy them.

"Fine. You've got it."

For some reason, he was disappointed. He changed the subject. "Are you ready for dinner?"

"The question is, are you?" He stood and started toward the door, noting she had left him to navigate on his own. After the first few hesitant steps he realized he knew the path. Relief surged through him at this small piece of independence. "What do you mean, am I?"

"I'm going to upgrade your meals. Tonight we're having roast beef, mashed potatoes and carrots. You'll be using a knife and cutting your own food."

Miffed at her tone he said, "I think I'm capable of that."

"Oh? Hmm...well, I'm glad to hear that, since yesterday you weren't capable of eating your breakfast."

Oh, she was in rare form, he noted. She enjoyed angering him, challenging him with that anger she created. But it wasn't going to work this time. It felt good to let go of the anger for just a little while. "But with your help I'm discovering so much," he taunted softly. "I'm learning by leaps and bounds, wouldn't you say?"

He knew she was thinking about earlier and grinned. Two could play the game she was playing. Finally she replied, her voice just a little higher than normal. "I'd say you're doing just fine."

He had started down the stairs before he consciously realized what she had done. "Keeping my mind busy so I can't balk at what you're doing?"

She laughed, another one of those sweet tinkling sounds. "Very good, Mr. Stevens. It usually takes my patients longer to realize that my chatter has a reason behind it.''

The musky, woodsy smell of Max's cologne reached him. Remembering the news report, Rand said, ''Hello, Max. You should have joined us today at the pool. I'm sure Ms. Jefferson would have enjoyed that.''

There was only a short pause before Max replied. ''I had too much to do at the office. However, I heard all about the swim.''

He scowled. Just what had Elizabeth told Max?

''Maybe I'll join you next time.''

The smells of dinner drifted in from the breakfast room and Rand's stomach rumbled. It had been a long time since he'd actually been hungry. It felt good to have worked up an appetite.

He carefully seated himself. When dinner was served he began eating. It was hard, cutting his meat and not feeling conspicuously clumsy. The only saving factor was that Elizabeth didn't hang over him like others had. And she didn't cut up his food, like the last nurse. That had angered him more than anything. Instead, Max and Elizabeth were talking, ignoring him as if he weren't there.

''I told Mary what Rand suggested about the jewelry and she said it was perfect. She called down, had the new clothes that are going out tomorrow pulled and the dressers go to work on it. Signs are being printed by our art department. We'll have everything ready in two days. Rand was right about Mary's knowledge of the department.''

''Thank you,'' he cut in, tired of being ignored.

''You're welcome. I took it by the scowl you didn't want to be included in conversation.''

''I wasn't scowling.''

Max chuckled. "If you say so. So, Elizabeth, do you ever get any nights off?"

There was only a slight pause then she replied, "Occasionally. I try to work around my patient's schedule. After all, the patient and therapist usually need a break from each other or they end up driving each other up the wall. But I usually don't worry about it the first month, until after a routine is established. As Rand can tell you, it takes time to learn a routine."

"Not at all, Elizabeth. I feel our routine is well established. Feel free to take any night you wish. After all, my brother is paying you for your time. As a matter of fact," he said, sudden jealousy eating him, "Max, you ought to take some nights off, too. Go out to a movie or something."

Elizabeth laughed, but it was unsteady, as if she was embarrassed or maybe nervous. "If you think we've got a routine, Rand, I need to inform you that we haven't even started yet. I've given you a few days to get used to me. I am planning on starting our first real day of work tomorrow."

Rand scowled, thoroughly exasperated that his brother hadn't replied to the taunt he'd flung out. "Well, then, that leaves you with tonight free."

Unable to sit there not knowing what looks were passing between Max and Elizabeth, he tossed down his napkin and stood. "If you'll excuse me. I need to get some sleep." He strode from the room.

"Well." Elizabeth raised surprised eyebrows. Turning her gaze to Max, she looked quizzical. "What did I say?"

Max grinned. "It wasn't you. It was my question about your nights."

It was Elizabeth's turn to scowl. "I thought I made it

clear to you when I took this job that I didn't get involved with patients.''

Max laughed. ''Rand didn't think you were talking about him. He thought you were contemplating going out with me.''

She knew her jaw sagged, which only made Max laugh harder. ''Am I that bad a catch?''

''I don't want a catch.''

He hooted. ''Oh, my dear, spoken like a true single woman of the nineties.''

''No. Spoken like a badly burned woman of the nineties,'' she blurted, then wished she could have called back that private information.

Max sobered. ''I'm sorry. I didn't know.''

''It's not something I discuss with my clients—or their families,'' she said wryly.

''Can I ask what happened?''

''Why?''

''It might explain why you just reacted so harshly at the suggestion of something other than friendship with a man.''

She shrugged. She hated it when anyone asked. She couldn't tell them the whole story, so she settled for a brief explanation, totally devoid of any of the shocking details. ''We were almost married. It didn't work out. I broke it off.''

He frowned. Finally accepting she wasn't going to tell him, he nodded. ''I don't think it's going to matter to Rand that you've been engaged.''

''Well, that's fine. It doesn't matter to me what he thinks since I don't become involved with my patients.''

He shook his head. ''That's not going to matter, either.''

Suddenly nervous, fearing he might be right, she said, "At least I'm forewarned."

"I didn't mean it like that. You sound like you're preparing for a battle."

"It sounds like I have to."

She tossed her napkin on the table and stood.

"Maybe you do," Max said coolly. "But let me add that Rand is very good at sieges."

She shrugged and walked toward the door, planning to go to her room. "As they say, the best defense is a good offense."

He grinned at the slightly skewered quote. "We'll see, Elizabeth Jefferson."

"Yes, we will. Good night." She strode off, feeling confident and ready for battle.

Heading up the stairs, though, her confidence faded. She was afraid Rand might just have what it took to get under her defenses and win any siege. For it wasn't the anger, or the determination, or the jealousy that attracted her, but the tenderness she knew his heart still possessed despite how battle-scarred it was.

And that scared her more than anything, because if her defenses were lowered, even for a short time, she was afraid all her secrets and fears would come pouring out.

She closed the door of her bedroom, crossed and sank onto her bed. She couldn't afford to let those secrets out, so she'd just have to make sure nothing developed from their professional relationship.

Glancing toward the ceiling, she whispered, "And that's the way I want it, God."

But she fearfully wondered if He didn't have an

agenda all His own, that didn't follow what she wanted this time.

She was afraid she would soon find out.

Chapter Six

"Good morning!" Elizabeth sang out the words several days later as she sailed into Rand's bedroom and headed for the drapes.

A groan issued from the bed, then a groggy voice. "Wha' time izit?"

"How many elephants can you fit in a car?"

"Huh?"

"Four. Two in the front seat, two in the back." Elizabeth jerked open the drapes then pushed open the balcony doors.

"I thought you were going to stop telling jokes."

"Oh, no, Rand. I only said no more chicken jokes."

Another groan was emitted. "You didn't answer my question. What time is it?"

"Six o'clock."

"What!" He sat straight up in bed and Elizabeth grinned.

"I told you we start a new routine this week. And that routine will begin with us up at six. From what Max says, you were usually up earlier."

"Max has a big mouth."

He looked so adorable, rumpled hair and whiskers. Absently he rubbed his chest, then realizing he didn't have a top on, he scowled. "Don't I get any privacy?"

"Sure. I'll meet you out on the balcony in five minutes."

"The balcony?"

She saw alarm on his face. "Don't worry. I'm not planning on pushing you off. Everyone needs to know at least two exits from each room. You've conquered the hallway, so I decided it was time to memorize this one. Besides, I wanted to watch the sun rise. That's a good way to start the day."

"The sun has already risen."

Her eyes widened. "Now how do you know that?" she teased.

He paused. "The sun is always up before six. Remember, I'm a morning person."

She laughed and headed out the doors. Rand had kept his distance since the pool and had grudgingly set himself to learn some basic things. Elizabeth was very happy with his progress, but edgy, too. She wasn't sure why, but decided it must be the unresolved tension between them.

She was attracted to him.

Embarrassingly so.

And she didn't like it. She had a past that was too painful to remember, and Rand's accidental touches couldn't help but stir up those memories.

Still, she wouldn't give up working with Rand. On his good days he was wonderful to be around. It was like looking at the world with new eyes whenever he got started talking about some discovery.

In minutes he came out, a robe over his chest, pajama

bottoms showing underneath. She inhaled deeply. "What do you smell?"

His mouth twisted. "Nothing."

"Well, then, I'll have to make an appointment with your doctor. Obviously you have sinus problems."

"Ha. Ha."

"Try again."

Rand reached out until he found the railing, his hands curling around it for protection. When he'd edged close to Elizabeth and felt safe, he turned his attention to his senses. Sniffing, he separated out the smells. A soft smile crossed his face. "Lilacs. My wife planted them when we first remodeled the house. I didn't know they were in bloom."

"What else?" Elizabeth asked softly.

"Grass. Someone cut the grass yesterday. It smells fresh, wet."

"And what do you hear?"

"Besides you and your awful jokes?" he asked, and she grinned.

"Yeah. Besides that."

He tilted his head. "Birds singing."

"Do you know what type?"

He paused for a minute. "No," he finally said.

Just then a bird started to sing in a nearby tree. "That's a blue jay. Listen." It repeated its call several times before a loud, obnoxious sound interfered.

"What's that?"

"A mockingbird. They tend to be very loud."

He chuckled. "Wait. That was a turtledove, wasn't it?"

She saw the excitement on his face at the distinctive sound. "See? You know more than you realize."

Just then he sniffed. "I smell...bacon?"

She laughed. "Indeed. Downstairs on the patio the cook has set up breakfast. Come on."

He reached out and took her elbow and then counted each step down. Elizabeth smiled as his lips moved slightly. She was so busy glancing over her shoulder, she missed a step. She stiffened and windmilled, trying to catch her balance. Just as she was sure she was going to take an awful spill, warm arms closed about her and jerked her against a hard chest.

"Are you okay?" His voice rumbled against her ear. "What happened?"

Hearing the growing concern in Rand's voice she said, "I turned to watch you and tripped."

A slow smile curved his lips. "Watch me, huh?"

She blushed and was glad he couldn't see it. "That's not what I meant."

"If you say so."

She didn't comment, only turned and finished her descent. Breakfast passed easily despite the jump of awareness between them.

"Now what?" Rand asked, pushing his plate back. He lifted his chin, his face turning toward the warmth of the rays of the sun.

"Feels like it's going to be a warm day, doesn't it?"

"Yeah," he murmured. "Are there clouds?"

"No. Despite this is the month of spring showers, it's been unusually dry. Now, let's get back to your previous question. As to now what, we go to your bedroom."

She blushed at his grin. "And you know I didn't mean *that* the way it sounded."

"Darn," he whispered.

"Very funny," she retorted. "You're going to learn how to sort through your clothes so you can get dressed by yourself. I'm tired of picking out your clothes."

His smile faded. "I can't do that."

"Sure you can." She stood. "Come on."

Going up the way they came, she waited until he was inside before opening his armoire. "I'm rearranging your clothes, dark to light, suits, pants, blazers then tops."

"A lot of good that'll do. Or have you forgotten, I can't see?"

"Can you touch?"

"Of course, but it won't help me see colors."

"A lot you know," she taunted. "Come here."

Hearing the sound of hangers cease, he knew she'd finished her rearranging. He approached. She reached down and took his hand. Her touch sent warm tingles up his arm, but he didn't comment. He was too upset. He didn't like feeling a fool. And he was definitely feeling that.

"Just like this morning. Let's explore our world. What do you feel?"

Her soft, quiet words urged him to reach out, explore, and despite the fear that he was going to screw up, he did just that. "Rough cloth...tweed. I take it this is one of my tweed blazers?"

"Very good."

"But which one? My gray or brown?"

Suddenly she was handing him a piece of paper. It reminded him of those huge sale price tags in some furniture stores. Five-sided, but more of a square with a circle cut out. "Is this a Do Not Disturb sign?" he asked.

"Not quite." He realized he'd embarrassed her again. Then he realized what she thought he was thinking. He grinned. "Just what are you thinking?" she asked.

"You wouldn't want to know."

"I'm sure. No, this is not a door sign. Feel the front."

He moved his hand over the flat surface and was surprised to feel raised lines. Carefully he traced them. It took two tries before he made it out. "B and R."

"That's right. Brown. We'll put that on the hanger. From now on you'll know that is your brown tweed blazer."

The first niggling of hope touched his heart. "We're going to do this for all of my clothes?"

"Yes. You see, they make these special pens that let you write anything you want and leave behind a thick enough line that you can trace it. I usually mark BK for black, BR for brown, GR for gray and so on. I've made up cards for the food containers in the kitchen so if you get hungry you can identify what you're getting ready to put in the microwave. Cards have been put on the outside of the cabinets, since Sarah says you don't go in there a lot. That way you can find what you need."

That hope was crushed by frustration. "I don't want my whole house rearranged."

"I realize that," she said quietly, and he felt ashamed for yelling at her and taking that bouncy, jubilant sound out of her voice. "But you do want to be independent again, don't you?"

Not if it means losing you, he thought and immediately felt appalled. "Of course," he said instead. It was simply that she was the first person to penetrate that inner darkness of his that made him think such a thing, he assured himself.

"Then small adjustments will be made. We won't attack the kitchen for a week or two. Right now you need to know your bedroom front and back. You need to learn your clothes. Your office needs to be memorized—"

"My office? Why?"

"The same reason. You want to be independent,

right? Well, you'll need to get back to work sooner or later."

He was overwhelmed by her words. It was impossible, wasn't it? But she was saying he was going to have a life again. He pictured someone blind as useless, pitied by their relatives and friends, wheeled off to sit on a bench all day long feeding pigeons. But this was not the picture she was painting.

He was suddenly a little scared of all she was saying. As if sensing his mood, she said, "We'll take it slowly. We don't want to dump everything on you at once. It's going to take months to learn all of this, to adjust to your surroundings and your new way of life. We won't go on until you are sure you're ready. Right now, let's concentrate on your room. When we're done here, I have a surprise for you."

"What?"

"Now if I told you, it wouldn't be a surprise, would it?"

Rand discovered that in his bathroom there were now two hampers. The one on the right was for whites. The one on the left was for darks. When he asked about his colored underwear and his white underwear she had no answer. Therefore, hearing her discomfort, he told her he could easily toss his white underwear and not have to worry about it any more. He loved her reaction to that. She told him Max could help.

An alarm clock, one he could feel the hands on, was brought in and replaced his old one. But when she gave him the electronic talking address and phone number book and the watch Max had purchased, he balked.

"Have you ever thought your brother might feel guilty?" she questioned quietly.

"Guilty?" He was flabbergasted. "For what? I was driving that night. He wasn't even there."

Elizabeth sighed. "For retaining his sight while you lost yours."

Rand had never thought of that. Now he did. "But he shouldn't feel that way."

"You're saying you never resented him for not losing his sight?"

Rand suddenly remembered some past conversations, even one prayer shouted out in anger. He cursed.

"That's normal, Rand. Max understands your feelings. He knows while you were going through your anger that sometimes in your darkest moments you wondered why. You as much said it to me when you asked me if I was going to take the *better* brother. Remember? I just thought maybe you ought to know how Max felt, too. He says you two haven't talked as much since the injury. He misses you."

Rand felt his insides twist. "I miss him, too," he finally admitted.

"Why don't you call him? Thank him for the watch and address keeper."

"I haven't used the phone..."

"Well, it's no different than before. Go ahead, call him. I need to go get that surprise."

She left. He didn't hear her leave, but her presence was gone. Only the lingering smell of her perfume remained.

He hadn't realized those bottled-up feelings were there. He'd say that Elizabeth was a mind reader if he believed in it. She was evidently a good guesser. Of course, there was one other option, and that was that God had sent her. But as he wasn't talking to God anymore, he doubted that.

He made his way to the bed and sank down on the side. He found the phone and realized that it was just as easy to dial it now as it had been. The number was in his head, and the familiar feel of the number pad was reassuring.

"Mr. Stevens's office."

He recognized Jennifer's voice immediately, although it had been over a year since he'd talked to her. "Jennifer, this is Rand. Is my brother in?"

"Mr. Stevens?" *Shocked* would describe her voice. "Geez, I didn't know you could use a phone. Uh, I mean—oh, geez, I'm sorry. Just a minute."

What did using a phone have to do with being blind? Then it struck him as funny that he would be condemning the girl when he had avoided it himself.

"Rand?"

"You don't have to sound so incredulous, Max. I'm blind, not crippled."

Rand knew where he'd heard that before, and winced to be quoting Elizabeth.

"Well, sure, brother, I know that. I just didn't know *you* knew that."

Rand laughed like he was supposed to. "Very funny. I uh, well, Max, I called to thank you for the watch and talking phone book."

Silence reined, and then Max's voice, sounding gruff, came back on the line. "Don't worry about it, Rand. I mean, hey, you're my brother. I wanted to get something you needed. I didn't know if you'd like it, though."

Max had never sounded unsure of himself. He'd always been very easygoing, taking life as it came. When had he changed? Rand was sure he knew the answer. His heart unbent and opened just enough to let Max in.

"I like them...a lot. You'll have to help me dredge up some phone numbers to put in the book."

Max laughed. "Hey, I have a few you might want to add."

"I don't think I want those kind," he joked, and realized how much he'd missed his easy camaraderie with his brother. "Thanks. Well, look, I gotta go. Eli—Ms. Jefferson is working me like a slave. We've reorganized my entire room—at least it feels that way—and she's got a dozen more things planned, I'm sure. I just wanted to say thanks."

"Okay. See you at home tonight."

"Yeah. At supper."

He placed the phone in the cradle. A burden he hadn't realized he'd been carrying rolled off his shoulders. He felt lighter, like a wall had come down that he hadn't realized had been erected. A smile of satisfaction spread across his face.

"Looks like you had an interesting conversation. Are you *sure* it was your brother you were talking to?"

"And just who else would it be?" he asked, his voice light.

"That's what I'm wondering." Before he could comment, she changed the subject. "Are you ready for your surprise?"

He shrugged despite the growing excitement. "Sure. What is it?"

He heard her approach. She was carrying something that made her tread sound heavier. A large box was plopped onto his lap. He automatically reached out and wrapped his arms around it. Feeling the wooden structure, he immediately recognized it. Sniffing, he smelled chicken. "A picnic basket?" he asked, wariness replacing the lighthearted moment. "And what I am supposed to do with this?"

"Why, take me on a picnic, of course."

Chapter Seven

"I'd rather have lunch on the balcony, if you don't mind."

"Oh, no. Max told me about a creek down through the woods. We just have to go there."

Elizabeth saw the fear flash across Rand's face before it became impassive again.

"Tell me what you're feeling," she said. "Don't bottle it up."

He debated then gave in. "I don't want to go through the woods. What if we get lost? It's been years since I went down there."

"Don't worry. I've walked the path already. It's very easy to follow."

"But what if something happens to you? I couldn't find my way back. You could be injured—"

"Don't borrow trouble. The path leads through the woods beyond the garden gate. The cook and butler both know where we're going. There's nothing to worry about."

She knew there was for him. He had confined himself

to this room for so long that leaving it had become a major hurdle. He'd overcome a small part by learning to eat meals downstairs again, and now she was asking him to try something more. "I'll be with you. I *am* your therapist. I wouldn't push you to do something that you weren't ready for."

He sighed and raked a hand through his hair. "I can't explain how hard this is," he finally said. "I've always been in control." He turned his face away, and she knew he was remembering the accident. "But it was suddenly all snatched away." He sighed again. "I mean, in a way that's fine. Look what my control got me last time—my wife's death."

"No, Rand," she whispered.

"Yes, Elizabeth. It did. I had to do everything my way, and my wife always let me. One of the only times she argued with me was about her fear of driving in the rain. She didn't want to go that night. I waved it off, telling her I could handle it. It ended up costing her her life." His gaze drifted in her general direction, and she could see the pain of memories echoed in his face. "Sometimes I think my penance for her death is losing all control."

"Are you afraid to take control of your own life?" she questioned carefully.

He turned toward the balcony windows, his gaze blank as he thought. Finally, he said, "I don't know. I never expected to have control of any part of my life again. And now, here you are, offering it to me. You know, maybe in my own life I can handle it, but you're asking me to risk your life, too."

"I don't understand."

"Going down to the creek with you. If something

happens, it would be up to me to get help. I don't know if I can deal with that. All right?''

She lifted surprised eyebrows at his honesty. Most people wouldn't have admitted that. ''Fine. We'll set a time limit to be back. I'll leave word that if we aren't back in three hours, then Timms is to come looking for us. Okay?''

''I don't really like it, but I have a feeling you won't take no for an answer.''

She grinned. ''You got that right.''

''Then it looks like we're going on a picnic.''

''Yes!'' she shouted, and he could feel the movement and hear the rustling of clothes as she danced around in front of him. A reluctant smile curved his lips.

''I just love picnics,'' she chattered as they headed out of his room.

Holding her elbow so he could hold it with one hand while he carried the hamper with the other, she blithely continued, oblivious to his fears or uncertainties...or maybe just ignoring them, he thought wryly.

''I used to love to go on picnics when I was a kid. We'd go to a park and eat, then play on the jungle gym. I was always a tomboy. I broke my right arm when I fell off one of those things. It was the last time Mom let me go on it. Told me I was twelve and shouldn't walk on top of the bars. It was time for me to find something else to do.''

''And did you?'' he couldn't resist asking.

''Yeah. I took up skateboarding, until I broke a leg.''

A picture was developing here, he though wryly. ''What then?''

''I took up bike riding. I was fifteen. Broke a collarbone, so my mom said no more motorbikes. When I was seventeen I took up judo.''

"Judo? Let me guess, you broke something then, too?"

"No." Her voice quieted. "My mom and dad were both killed in an auto accident. I had to drop it."

"I'm sorry."

"Don't be. It was a long time ago."

"So you decided after all of these accidents to become a therapist?"

"Something like that."

He heard the hesitation in her voice, but before he could ask, she said, "So, you know my life story. What about you? As a child, were you accident-prone, too?"

He laughed. "No. Never broke a bone my entire childhood."

At the back gate she paused to push it open. A loud creak resounded. "You need to oil that. Not a one? Not even a finger or toe? I kicked a toe once on a couch, by accident, you understand, and was in a walking shoe for six weeks."

"No. I had a very sedate life. Now, on the other hand, Max was quite a collector of cuts and bruises."

"Oh?" He heard the suspicion. "And why was that?"

He laughed. "I was the one always coming up with the schemes—"

"And he was the one who carried them out," she finished.

"You got it. And some weren't so smart."

"Like what?"

"Well, there was the one where I had a crush on the girl next door. I decided to serenade her."

"How old were you?"

"Thirteen."

"Geez."

"Tell me about it. Max only played the piano, though,

while I played the guitar and horn. So I told him I would play the instrument and he could sing the song for me, on her trellis.''

''And he actually did it for you?''

''Only after I offered him my allowance for the month.''

''So, what happened?''

''The trellis didn't hold up under the added weight.''

''Oh, no.'' She giggled. ''Poor Max.''

''Poor Max? He may have broken an arm. But I was grounded for a month, and the girl, impressed with Max's antics, started dating him, instead!''

She laughed, her voice sounding right at home in the forest. And in the forest they were, he suddenly realized. The old dirt path was partially grown over with grass. He could feel it brushing his pants legs.

''So, tell me what you hear, what you feel, what you smell,'' she said as they continued, her laughter subsiding.

''Is every moment with you a lesson?''

''Of course not. I'm a nature lover. I try to make all my patients develop a love for it.''

''Yeah, uh-huh,'' he said, but did as she said. Slowly, the sounds and smells came to him. ''Birds. There are several different types. Some loud and harsh, others soft and musical. I'd never noticed that before.'' He paused, then said, ''The wind blowing through the pine trees makes the needles rattle. The sound sorta reminds me of sandpaper running across a smooth piece of wood.''

''How do you know the trees are pine?''

He grinned. ''Even if I didn't know my own backyard, I can smell them. They have a very strong odor.''

''What else do you smell?''

Your perfume, a scent all your own that is the essence

of you. But he didn't say that. Instead, he said, "Dirt. Decay. It's a little disorienting walking here."

"How about the sun? Do you feel it?"

His eyes widened. "Occasionally. There must be breaks in the trees."

"There are."

"I don't remember that."

They walked in companionable silence for a few minutes. "You have any other feelings?" she asked.

Desire, he thought. *A longing to know you better.* But he couldn't say that, either, so instead he said, "I feel a peace that I never realized I associated with the forest. I always thought of the forest as a quiet place, somewhat eerie, but I think, instead, it's very noisy, very alive, giving me all kinds of clues to what it hides within its depths."

He could hear the smile in her voice as she said, "Yes, it is alive, communicating with its own language if you only take the time to listen to what it is saying."

"That's why you brought me here, isn't it?"

"One reason. Sometimes when you're isolated you forget how to live. Getting out and remembering that God created all things living reminds you how special life is."

He stiffened. "I'd rather not discuss that, if you don't mind."

"What?"

"God," he said tersely.

"But— Fine."

He felt he had let her down but he couldn't help it. He could *not* face God right now. Too many things had happened. He didn't want to forgive and forget. If he faced God, he knew God would want that from him. And he wasn't going to do it.

The agreeable silence continued between them until they neared the water. "Hear it?" she asked.

"Uh-huh." He could smell it, too.

The ground sloped downward as they neared the slow-trickling stream. "It swells during rains. Despite how low it is now, it's never run dry that I know of."

Elizabeth took the picnic basket from him and spread the blanket. Awkwardly, Rand seated himself on the edge of it.

"It looks like Sarah was very comprehensive when she packed. Iced tea," she said, pulling out a small jug, "ham sandwiches, pickles, olives, cherry tomatoes and oh, yum, strawberries!"

Rand chucked. Despite his insecurities, he enjoyed Elizabeth's company. Over the last few days he realized Elizabeth wasn't going to say anything about his grace-less mistakes unless she was teasing him. She was patient, easygoing, occasionally joking about something he'd never allow anyone else to show even a hint of humor at, like his silly mistakes. But it was never done so it would hurt, but more like the time he'd locked his tie in his desk drawer at work—with it still around his neck. Max had hooted when Rand had nearly choked himself. And so had Rand. That had been over two years ago.

Or maybe the reason he didn't mind was that Elizabeth joked about herself, as well, when he could get her to talk about herself. "I take it by the enthusiasm in your voice you like strawberries?" he asked.

"Oh, yes," she said and then grinned. "Hey, why'd the strawberry marry the banana?"

"Not *another* one," he said.

"Come on, guess."

Rand sighed, knowing she expected him at least to

put up a little fuss. With a facade of reluctance, he said, "I don't know...maybe because they fell for each other?"

Elizabeth giggled. "Wrong, though a good one. The strawberry thought the banana had appeal!"

Rand groaned loudly, then let out a low chuckle, which sent Elizabeth into another round of giggles.

She had a beautiful laugh.

Rand adjusted himself until his back was comfortably against the oak tree under which they sat.

He dreamed of her laughter at night. And even in the morning and afternoon when he was awake he absorbed the peace it brought him. When he felt alone, closed off in some dark place where no one could reach, reliving the nightmare of losing so much that had been so dear to him, Elizabeth's laughter would float to him on the wind, bringing peace and tranquility—and longing.

He had to admit it, whether he wanted to or not. There was a longing inside him to share that happiness and taste the joy of living again. He was so tempted to reach and grab that elusive feeling that fluttered about him, teasing him with its closeness, only to flit off when he remained impassive.

But he just couldn't.

If he reached out and found that it was all a dream, there was really nothing there to hold on to, he didn't know if he could survive the blow. And if it was real? He didn't know if he could survive that, either.

He heard the crinkling of plastic wrap and then Elizabeth pressed a plate into his hands. A cup with a lid and straw followed.

He set the cup next to him and ran his fingers over the plate until he found where everything was located. "What, no strawberries for me?"

"For dessert. You be a good boy and you'll get some."

"I'm not a boy," he said.

Elizabeth smiled. "No. You certainly are not a boy and haven't been for quite some time," she quipped.

Elizabeth watched the ease with which he devoured his food, pleased. She made short work of her own food, too. Talking with Rand was soothing when he was in this mood. It was nice to be able to let down her guard, something she hadn't done in a long time. She loved to joke and laugh and enjoyed it when Rand joined in.

"You know," she said, after taking a gulp of tea to wash down the last of her sandwich, "if you keep making this type of progress, you will be ready for your first outing soon. I still wish you would train with the cane first."

"I told you, I don't want a stick."

He had thrown a fit when his custom-made walking stick had arrived at the house, insisting he didn't want it.

"Well, be that as it may, before our sessions are over, you will either know how to use a stick or own a dog."

"No dog."

"Then the stick it is," she said airily, having been over the argument of a dog many times, as well.

"What about the strawberries?" Rand asked, changing the subject. He handed her his empty plate and stared in her direction, waiting.

She sighed. No use continuing on any subject when Rand got that look on his face. He could be very stubborn at times. "Okay, strawberries it is, but you're gonna have to earn them."

"Oh?" he asked, raising an eyebrow, looking as arrogant as his brother had yesterday when they'd been cornered by some reporters in town.

"Tell me a joke."

"Forget it." His jaw turned stubborn.

"Just one joke," Elizabeth wheedled.

He wavered, and Elizabeth hoped he was finally going to reach out and join in the fun. Instead, his face hardened. "Never mind."

He put his hands on either side of his legs and started to push himself up. Elizabeth thought quickly, realizing she'd pushed too hard. Grabbing a strawberry, she twisted off the green stem and held it in front of him. "Spoilsport," she said in a pouty voice.

Rand stilled, feeling the strawberry against his lips. He could feel Elizabeth's breath against his cheek and realized she was leaning over right in front of him. Attraction spiraled within him, stunning him with its intensity.

When she prodded his lower lip, he didn't argue but opened his mouth and took a bite of the sweet red fruit. Juice dribbled down his chin, but before he could catch it, Elizabeth's finger scraped across his stubbled jaw, collecting the juice.

She started to pull back but Rand stopped her. Gently, he tugged on her hand, pulling it forward until he could slip her index finger into his mouth. He sucked gently, licking off all the juice she'd caught.

He heard her suck in a sharp breath and suddenly he realized what he was doing. This wasn't his wife. This was a woman who worked for him, his therapist. And no matter how attracted he felt to her, he couldn't do something like that to a woman who, for all practical purposes, was really still a stranger.

"Forgive me," he said, huskily.

She didn't answer, only pressed another strawberry into his hand. "Your turn," she finally said. He was relieved he hadn't offended her. Instead, hearing the husky note in her voice made him think the desire must be mutual.

He pulled the green stem off and then, with his right hand, he reached out until he cupped her head. He eased her forward, his thumb tracing her cheek until he encountered her lips.

They were parted, waiting. He would have liked to kiss her, but knew that was not what she'd meant when she'd said *your turn.* Instead, he pressed the strawberry into her mouth. Her lips closed over the tip of his index finger temporarily, then it was released.

"Payback," she said, though it sounded shaky.

He realized they were both playing at a game he wasn't sure he was ready for. So he backed off.

"You like picnics?" he asked, leaning against the tree, turning his head toward the sound of the lapping water.

"Yeah," she said, and though her voice wasn't as bouncy as normal, the breathy quality was gone from it. "I always had a vision of one day meeting the right man who would take me on a picnic."

"Right man?" Rand questioned, hearing the smile in her voice.

"You know, the one who would go hang gliding with me and parachuting. Those types of things. I had this vision of us being in a plane on a picnic."

"On a plane?" Rand asked, certain she was teasing him.

"Yes. On a plane. We'd have those little cute sandwiches they serve at parties, and strawberries, and then, wearing parachutes, we'd jump out of a plane. We'd

land in a large field near a pond. There would be trees
there. We'd take off our parachutes and sit down under
one of those trees. The man would lie back, his head in
my lap, and we'd watch the ducks out on the pond, just
sit in silence and watch.''

He chuckled. ''Quite a dream.''

''That's why it's a dream. I'll never find someone
crazy enough to do that.'' It was said simply, so simply
that he knew she believed it.

Saddened, he said, ''Maybe you'll find that man one
day, get engaged—''

''Been there, done that,'' she quipped.

Confused, he said, ''I thought you said it was a
dream?''

''That part, yes. The engagement, no.''

''You're engaged?''

She laughed, though it was strained. ''Of course not.
I wouldn't be living in with patients if I was. No, I was
engaged. No big deal. It happened a long time ago.''

He heard something in her voice. ''That's not what
your tone says.''

''I think you're hearing things,'' Elizabeth said, and
though her voice rang with a light warning, he ignored
it. This was the most she'd opened up since he'd met
her and he wanted to know more.

''Come on, I share my feelings with you all the time,''
he said, though he knew what he was asking of her was
different. He should have realized if Elizabeth was cornered she would fight back.

But he hadn't expected it. Nor had he expected her to
destroy their easy mood with one simple sentence. ''But
I'm not the patient.''

Confounded, anger slowly simmering, Rand gaped at her as she suddenly stood and began to gather up the discarded trash.

She turned the car slowly, annoying Rand again at her as she suddenly... and began to follow at the drunken pair.

Chapter Eight

Elizabeth pulled up in the large driveway well past midnight.

She was miserable.

Today had been a disaster. After her rude remark to Rand, he had erupted like Mount Saint Helens on a bad day.

Of course, she couldn't blame him. She had gone out of her way to make sure Rand felt comfortable with her, doing everything she could think of to lower those protective walls that he kept between them.

She hadn't expected the attraction between them to overwhelm her, though, when they were on their picnic. And when he started questioning her personal life, she had struck back in the first way she could think of—she had thrown up her wall of patient versus nurse.

She pulled her car into an empty slot behind the main house and killed the engine, then she banged her hands against the steering wheel as she again recalled the furious look on Rand's face.

How could she have done something so stupid? Then,

instead of clearing the air after their shouting match about personal information versus information necessary to helping him recover, she had stormed off.

She'd left word with Sarah that she was going out that evening, letting Sarah assume she had a date, when that was not at all the truth.

She'd gone by her apartment, changed into her slinky little "on the town" dress—as she thought of her satiny black thing with short capped sleeves—and then called her friend Molly to meet her at a ritzy restaurant for dinner.

After dinner she'd gone to the movies and then moped around for an hour before finally returning.

And in all that time the only conclusion she had come to was that she had to apologize for being such a jerk and hope she hadn't done irreparable damage to their working relationship. *Father, forgive me,* she whispered as she opened her door and grabbed her purse. *I've got such a temper sometimes.*

She slipped out of the car and trudged to the back door. Inserting the key Max had given her, she unlocked the door and slipped inside, quietly closing the door behind her. She quickly reset the security code and then headed up the wide staircase to her room.

No lights were on in Rand's room. Of course, that didn't mean anything. Rarely did he turn on a light. She should just go in and talk to him, but it was after midnight and she really didn't look forward to eating humble pie.

Instead, she went into her suite. Dropping her purse on the desk, she started toward her bedroom, reaching for her zipper as she went.

A hand closed over her arm.

Terror surged through Elizabeth, a long suppressed

fear left over from years ago when she had been running from her stalking ex-fiancé and he had enjoyed breaking in at night to scare her.

Whirling around, she jerked, intending to catch the intruder by surprise. But it didn't work. She was hauled against the large body.

Blood roared in her ears, blocking out all sound as she struggled.

The body propelled her backward, pushing her against the couch. "No!" she wailed, striking out, kicking, scratching, biting, bile rising in her throat.

She continued to fight until she realized the person above her, instead of hitting her or ripping at her clothes, was instead soothing her, his arms wrapped around her.

And he was no longer on top of her, but beside her, holding her close, her face buried in his neck, one large hand stroking her hair.

She trembled, reaction setting in even as she recognized Rand's voice. Instead of pushing him away, she burrowed closer, allowing his warmth to touch her, envelop her, reassure her. His lips touched her forehead, her cheeks, her ears before trailing gently to her lips. Then she was tucked against him and he again crooned nonessential words until she relaxed.

Finally, after what seemed like hours, he leaned away from her. "I didn't mean to startle you," he said.

She laughed, sounding battle weary. "Startle, huh?"

"Well, I didn't want to overstep the boundaries you set up this afternoon."

Elizabeth pushed away. "About that..."

"It's okay, Elizabeth."

"No, it's not." She sat up, scooting over and allowing Rand to sit by her. "I was wrong. I have some personal hang-ups from the past and I don't discuss them much."

"I can see why," he murmured with a gentleness that brought tears to her eyes. She knew he was attributing what had just happened to her past.

"I take it your ex-fiancé's name was Michael."

She gasped.

"I'm not a mind reader. You called out his name when you were fighting me."

She was glad at that moment he couldn't see her. She was certain she had turned deathly white. "It was a long time ago, almost ten years. He was very possessive and didn't let go of me very easily."

"What happened?"

She hesitated then shrugged. When she did, she felt his arm behind her on the couch. That small touch gave her the courage to say what needed to be said. After all, hadn't she been berating herself earlier for staying so closed up? Not all men were like Michael. And she would soon be gone from here. What could it hurt to tell him? "I thought I was doing the right thing, trying to work out the problems before I finally broke it off. I had invested so much time, but he just got more and more possessive. When he flew into a rage one night because I spent time with a few women friends, I realized I couldn't go through with the wedding. I broke it off."

He waited.

She sucked in a shaky breath. "He didn't like the idea of losing me. I woke up in the hospital in traction from a broken femur as well as internal injuries. Of course, there were some friends who tried to tell me since the wedding was less than a week away I shouldn't bail out. It was only my nerves and my fall down the stairs that were causing the sudden fears."

"Your friends censured you for breaking it off?"

She shrugged. "You know how some people feel

about commitment. Unfortunately, the people I knew told me I shouldn't leave no matter what. They said Michael was such a nice young man. Of course, they'd never seen his possessiveness or cruelty.''

"After what he did to you? I wouldn't call them friends." His voice shook with emotion. He couldn't believe how calmly she sat there and told him about the abuse she had lived through. Yet it was the very calmness that told him how painful her memories were.

With a careful breath, he scooted closer to offer silent support.

"They believed his story that I had fallen down the stairs. He had never marked me up bad," she said, as if it mattered. "It was always during the middle of an argument. He would suddenly explode and push me or...whatever." She shrugged. "I mean, I usually only ended up a little sore, never anything bad."

"Don't make excuses for him," Rand said, his voice vibrating with rage on her behalf.

"I guess old habits die hard," she said, then sighed, relaxing against the couch, needing to feel the brush of his arm against her again.

"It was unfortunate that I tried to leave when he told me not to. I think that's what pushed him over the edge. Looking back, I realize I shouldn't have confronted him alone. Anyway, he caught me at the top of the stairs."

"Well, I hope they threw the book at him," Rand muttered.

Relieved that he wasn't going to censure her, she said, "Actually, they didn't. As I said, no one had ever seen any marks on me before. The police had never been called until that night. When the case went to court it was ruled accidental."

"What!" Rand's whole body stiffened with shock.

"They made me out to be a whining girlfriend who had been jilted and who wanted to get back at the man who'd jilted her, so I claimed abuse instead of tripping down the stairs in a fit of pique."

"I can't believe—" he started only to be cut off harshly.

"Believe it. You'd be surprised some of the ridiculous problems women go through who are in abusive relationships."

"Is that why you are so leery of discussing your past?"

"Yes. I'm happy here in Baton Rouge. I've learned in other cities many times when people find out you've been abused they feed the gossip mills with it. You're shunned, stared at, pitied and worse."

Rand's heart was hurting. "How long did you date him?"

"Five years."

"Five years?" He wanted to shout, *How could you stay with a man like that!* Instead, he asked very calmly, "Why didn't you leave?"

"How do you get out of something like that," she demanded, "when the person won't let you go? You don't know how many times I tried to ease away, hoping we could end it amicably. But he would cry, tell me how much he loved me and beg me to help him work it out. He even suggested stress management and premarriage counseling once in desperation, which I decided against since Michael was such a private person. I should have listened to my instinct and gone. Though I doubt he would have followed through with his offer since he thought all counselors were just in it for the money."

She shifted again, and he realized how badly she needed to talk. Perhaps this afternoon had been the trigger, or maybe she just felt comfortable sitting here in the dark with him. He shifted closer, letting her feel his silent support, then realized if he kept moving closer, she was going to be in his lap! "Go on."

"I knew the relationship was strained, but I hadn't finished college and attributed our problems to that," she confessed in a small voice. "I've gone over this so many times in my head." She cleared her throat and said, her voice stronger, "I met Michael in my first year. He was wonderful, sweet, kind, needy."

She sighed and he felt the tension as she tried to un-obtrusively move closer...or maybe she wasn't even aware of her actions. He could feel her hands as she clasped and unclasped them. "I'm sure if I had gone to counseling, they could have helped me. But Michael convinced me not to go. Michael was sure we'd be fired from where we worked if they found out we were seeing shrinks, as he called them. It was a nightmare. And then, of course, there were those few people I talked with who thought Michael was such a sweet person and maybe it was my temper causing the problems." She sighed, a broken, defeated sound.

"I guess it was the fear of the unknown as well as the dependency on Michael that kept me in the relation-ship. I had never failed at anything before. How could I fail at something so important? Believe me, I never would have stayed had I realized it would cost me my ability to have children."

"What?" he asked sharply.

"The fall down the stairs—there was internal damage and scarring," she confided in a shaky voice. "The doc-tors said I'd probably never have children."

She began to weep softly and Rand gathered her in his arms. He wondered if this was the first time she had ever cried over her loss, then realized the enormity of the burden she had been carrying.

"You did what you could. I think maybe, sometimes, it's easy for someone to say give up everything, go, run away, start over again to a person who is living in a nightmare. I mean," Rand said, trying to say what was in his mind, "for instance, someone who has a good job and a nice house doesn't have to worry from one day to the next about food or shelter. And yet, if you told them to quit, move and start over with nothing, I wonder if they would do it? So, how much harder it must be for someone who is down in a deep hole of despair to see their way clearly."

Her weeping turned to sobs and she burrowed against him. And in that moment, a crack opened up in Rand Stevens's heart.

Here was someone who had been in worse shape than he had, and she had survived.

Eventually, her sobs quieted and she stilled.

"Were you in therapy?" he questioned, when she finally pulled away.

He heard her blow her nose and let out a watery sigh. "Yes. Physical therapy. I had months of retraining my leg. It wasn't an easy process. That's how I got into my work. But I wanted to work with the blind. Another patient in the hospital room with me is what made me choose this particular area to specialize in."

"I wondered how you had gotten into such work."

"And you, Rand?" she asked. "How did you get into the retail business?"

He chuckled. "Family owned and operated. I've always been a very organized person. I had my whole life planned out from the time I was six years old. Even had my wife picked out, the girl next door."

"Not the one Max serenaded?" she asked, astounded

"The very one. She dumped Max, went off to private school, came back and we married."

She laughed. "Poor Max. You won in the end, anyway."

The smile left his voice. "Yeah, I won."

"I'm sorry."

Her voice was soft, sincere. He knew she meant it. "So am I," he said, standing. "So am I."

When he reached the door, Elizabeth called out, "Why were you in here, Rand? Did you want something?"

"I just wondered how your date went."

He waited, then when she didn't answer, he opened the door. Just as he stepped into the hall, he heard her softly spoken words. "I didn't have a date, just a girlfriend and a movie."

He didn't comment, continuing to his room instead, but somehow his step was lighter than it had been earlier, and his hopes were buoyed.

Chapter Nine

Elizabeth pulled on her jeans and a soft wool short-sleeve sweater, all the while dreading going down for breakfast. She was embarrassed over last night. For Pete's sakes, she had cried all over—*all* over—her patient. And he had sat there and allowed it.

She groaned, a low sound. It had to be hormones making her act like such a ninny. "Dear Father," she began as she sat in front of the mirror, brushing her hair as if it was three feet long instead of its actual length, "You are going to *have* to help me keep my mouth shut around that man! I told him things I've only told You!" She tossed the brush down and spritzed herself with perfume.

Looking in the mirror, she sighed. "I've seen pictures of his wife. She was beautiful. Look at me. Besides, I will not trust a man again."

Do not look at yesterday for that day is gone, nor to the future, but today.

"Take it one day at a time," she muttered, thinking aloud. "But I don't want to take one day at a time with *any* man. And I'm totally blowing it. I have a feeling he hates You. What am I suppose to say to him? How am I supposed to reach him? I think I'm developing feelings for this man. What am I going to do?''

A knock at her door interrupted her. She went to her bed, scooped up her Bible and laid it on her nightstand. Straightening her vanity, she looked around once more. She was a stickler about keeping this room spotless. Heaven knew her own house wasn't ever this neat. Finally, she went to the door.

Why wasn't she surprised to find Rand there...and looking as grouchy as usual. ''Good morning,'' she sang out, opening the door wide. ''Since you're at my door instead of me at yours I can only surmise you are going to tell me a joke?''

He stepped into the room, hesitated, then stepped out. ''No. I came to tell you I'm going stir-crazy in this house. I want to get out today.''

Now *this* was a surprise. And here she'd thought she had totally messed up everything with this man. Would wonders never cease? Or maybe God had a little more influence in this man's life than she realized. ''Out? Out where?''

''I don't know. It's Saturday. Do you know any places that aren't crowded? Maybe we can stop by the office and see Max.''

She knew she was gaping. She couldn't help it. Still, an idea formed. ''What goes up in the air white and comes down yellow and white?''

He frowned, then sighed. ''I don't know.''

''An egg. So how about it? Can I treat you to breakfast?''

''I don't know,'' he murmured, and she could see the banked fear in his eyes.

''Wear sunglasses, and we'll go somewhere there will

be no people, or very few. How's that? Then we can stop by the office around noon. Since your offices are not open on Saturday and anyone doing extra work will be gone, we should be unobserved.''

"Maybe this was a bad—"

"No! I won't take no for an answer. Come on. It's the least I owe you after a wild night out on the town without you.''

She immediately regretted bringing up last night. But to her surprise, Rand's features softened just the tiniest bit and he nodded.

"You picked out your own clothes today?" she asked, looking him over. He wore a pale peach shirt and tan slacks with a darker belt looped around his middle.

"Yes. A problem?"

"No.'' She started down the hall, Rand following. He no longer held onto her when they went through the house. Only a couple of times had he bumped a stray table. "Quite nice, actually,'' she said cheekily and breezed down the stairs, leaving a stunned Rand behind.

He wasn't sure what to make of Elizabeth's actions today. He'd tossed and turned most of the night, remembering her confession of pain and confusion, understanding a little better her wariness around him.

But today she acted as if nothing had happened. He could handle that fine, if his emotions weren't involved. But they were. He felt something for this woman and wanted to explore that.

However, she was acting like there was nothing there. Of course, it could have to do with him getting up on the wrong side of the bed.

He had been grouchy simply because he couldn't figure out just what emotions he was feeling for her. They were all tangled up with his therapy. He cared for her, but was it because she had brought him out of a pit of despair? Was it only because he was just now feeling alive again after getting over the pain of loss? Oh, he'd never forget or stop loving his wife, but he was no longer looking back.

Or maybe, just possibly, it was because she was an attractive woman. True, he couldn't see her in the conventional sense. But he found that a plus in some ways. She was tiny, well shaped—he'd found out just how well shaped as he'd held her against him last night while she'd cried. She was the type of woman a man felt the need to protect, to cherish. Especially after last night. But he wasn't sure she would want his concern or protection.

Rand, being a man always in total control, was at a loss over how to handle his seesawing emotions. Thus, when she had answered her door and the familiar scent of her perfume had swept over him, he'd snapped at her.

And she had ignored him like she had the first day. She had simply told a joke, flirted with him and then flitted off. Well, things weren't the same anymore, were they?

He growled low in his throat. If he had anything to say, things were *not* going back to how they were!

He went down the steps and found the front door where Elizabeth was waiting. "I had the car pulled around. Are you sure you won't consider a walking sti—"

"No! Absolutely not."

"You know, I'm not going to be here forever for you to lean on."

It was a warning, he was certain. He ignored her words. "Shall we go?"

They got in the back seat of the car, and Phil drove

off. "I just love this car. It was nice of Max to leave it behind today for us, don't you think?"

"Max is a nice guy," Rand said dryly.

"Oh, come on." She laughed, a deep, rich, husky sound that had Rand frowning. Did she have to sound so beautiful, too? "Don't you want to know where I'm taking you?"

He shrugged.

"How do you know I'm not kidnapping you, having you delivered to a plane so we can go parachuting together?"

A small smile curved his lips. "That would be just like you."

"Now, Rand," she admonished. "Actually, Rosie, a friend of mine, owns a restaurant near where you work. It doesn't open until noon, but I'm sure she'll let us in early."

"You sound pretty positive."

"Well, actually, I go there quite a bit when I'm in the area. So it won't be eggs for breakfast, but Italian."

"For breakfast," he said with no inflection in his tone.

"Yeah. I love Italian. However, if your stomach isn't up to it at ten in the morning..."

"I'll be fine," he said, wondering how in the world this woman could eat spicy this early. He had a feeling the cool, neat woman was only a facade. He would love to explore her apartment unannounced one day.

"What are you thinking?"

"That I must have been a fool to go out in public so soon."

"Actually, you aren't. I would have preferred you be a little more independent, but as you are going to two places that will be practically deserted, you couldn't ask for a better situation."

Just then the car pulled up to the curve in front of a small exclusive Italian restaurant. The driver came around and opened the door. Rand stepped out and then held his hand in the general direction of the car door.

Elizabeth took her cue and slipped her hand in his. She stepped out and stopped when she was just ahead of him. The way he took her elbow and followed her lead was so smooth she doubted anyone would realize this man was blind. "You're doing great. Mama Ria's is just ahead. Here's the door."

She felt his right hand slip up and snag the door as she swung it open. Once inside, Rosie came rushing over. "Rosie!" Elizabeth called out, giving her a brief hug. "This is my friend Rand. We were hoping you could let us sample today's specials."

Rosie laughed. She reached out and took Rand's hand. "As skinny as she is you would not know she comes in here about once a week to *sample* my specials. Go, find a seat. The eggplant parmesan is the special today. I'll bring it right out." She turned and headed toward the kitchen.

"Rosie is a wonderful woman," Elizabeth said, slowly weaving her way through the tables, giving Rand plenty of time to adjust his gait. "She's no taller than me though just about as round as she is tall. Sweet as can be. She started this business eight years ago. It's become very successful."

"I know. I've eaten here many times myself."

"Really? Well, I should have guessed, as close to your office as it is."

She stopped in front of a table for two that was set against the window overlooking the street. Rand turned his face to the window, the heat evident, then turned to

her. He assisted in seating her and then did a good job of feeling his way to his chair.

"She knew I was blind."

Elizabeth, who was putting her napkin in her lap, smiled. "Yes, she did. I've brought other patients here before. She's a dear, never blundering around embarrassing them. I hope you don't mind."

"I—"

"Here we are," Rosie said, bringing two plates and two glasses of water. A waiter behind her set down two glasses of tea and then, wishing them good eating, Rosie and the waiter were gone.

"She's in the middle of getting everything ready for lunch. Otherwise she would probably plop herself down and dig out your whole life story."

Rand nodded. He spread his napkin in his lap and picked up his fork and knife.

"Eggplant is on the left and there are spaghetti noodles on the right. Now spaghetti, that is going to be interesting." She laughed.

"Thanks for the vote of confidence."

"Well, it'll be a good learning experience. Don't worry. You're not being watched." She took a bite. "Mmm, this is good."

Rand used his fork and spoon to scoop up some noodles. He twirled them around, using his index finger as unobtrusively as possible to note when the spoon was against his finger and the noodles were gone. Thinking himself very ingenious, he put the fork in his mouth, and realized he could barely chew he had picked up so many noodles.

Elizabeth noticed. And instead of ignoring it the way he had hoped, she said, "At least you won't starve."

Frustrated, he set the fork down.

"Now don't go getting upset. Remember, things are different. I know it bothers you, but try not to worry. Just enjoy your meal. And if you come in here on your own you can order the veal or something else you feel more comfortable cutting up. No big deal."

"Maybe not to you."

"I understand, Rand. Just do your best and be glad we're alone."

Rand did his best, and was able to keep all the food off his shirt, or at least Elizabeth swore he had no food on him. It was not the most comfortable meal. As a matter of fact, after the meal, he was exhausted from the stress. Still, he wanted to go by work, show Max that he was getting out again. He still felt guilty after talking to Max and finding out just what his brother had been going through at the office.

They thanked Rosie and paid, or rather, Elizabeth paid. Rand fumed when he realized he didn't know how to figure out what was what when it came to money. Then they went out to where the car was waiting. "We'll work on folding your money. You just have to learn how to fold each denomination differently and then you can recognize it by feel."

She slipped her seat belt on and moved around until she was comfortable. "That wasn't so bad, was it?" Elizabeth asked softly.

"Awful," Rand stated. He slid into the car and ran his fingers through his hair. "I feel like I just ran the Boston Marathon."

"It'll get better." She patted his knee.

That was it. Rand reached out and snagged her wrist, pulling her forward. "Don't ever pat my knee again."

Elizabeth blinked, surprised by Rand. "Okay," she

said. "If it upsets you so, I won't do that. I don't know why—"

"I think you do," he murmured and pulling her against his chest, he kissed her, his mouth molding hers, gently exploring her lips until they were both breathless. When he could again speak, he said, "I'm not just some patient anymore, Elizabeth, and no matter how you treat me, it isn't going to make this thing between us go away."

"There's nothing between us," she whispered, feeling his rough hand as it caressed her jaw.

"There's something, good or bad I haven't decided. Neither have you, if the mixed signals you're giving out are any indication. Fine. I understand. Believe me, I do. But no more treating me like a little boy."

"I didn't mean to," she said, her voice trembling. She wasn't sure if it was from his nearness or the fact that she realized he was right.

"Just so you know," he said, his voice low and husky. Then he lowered his head and kissed her again, his lips soft and insistent on hers.

Finally, when she was sure she couldn't handle any more, he eased back. He leaned his head against the seat and closed his eyes. It was only then she noted the lines on his face.

He was very weary. She should have noticed that earlier, would have noticed it if she hadn't been so intent on not staring at him. "We can go home if you'd rather. The driver is just now at the parking lot."

"No." Rand opened his eyes and turned his face toward the door. "I want to visit Max."

"Of course," she murmured.

When the car stopped, Elizabeth slid out of her seat and waited outside the car for Rand to follow. They were in an underground garage near an elevator. She saw Max's car, and a special gate that required a card. The lot must be for the executives, she thought, surprised.

"Can anyone use this elevator?" she asked Rand as he touched her elbow.

"Just the top floor. This is express for top executives." Rand slipped his wallet from his pants pocket and started pulling out cards, feeling each one. He grumbled when he dropped some. Elizabeth bent and picked them up. "We'll have to organize this wallet when we get home. I'm sorry. Since I wasn't planning on taking you out this soon—"

"Don't apologize. It's my fault. I feel like a five-year-old."

"But you shouldn't."

His hand went over a card that was obviously the right one. He inserted it into the elevator and then waited. In minutes the car arrived and they stepped into it. Neither spoke as the car ascended.

But when the door opened, Elizabeth couldn't hold back her awe. "Wow! This is nice. Look at that carpet. I'd love to take my shoes off and walk through that. You know, I do that at home. When I'm in my suite I take my shoes off and walk barefoot back and forth just to feel the thick carpet."

Rand took her elbow. "Interesting. I'll have to come in and join you sometime," he murmured. She could feel his tension despite the joke he made.

But, since he did attempt a joke, she wickedly replied, "Want to join me right now?"

He chuckled like he was supposed to, which was good, because someone had just walked into sight. "Er, Rand, there's a girl, a blonde, maybe twenty, walking this way. She obviously recognizes you."

"Which direction is she coming from?"

"The left."

"Ah, Max's office. Must be Jennifer."

"Hello, Rand?"

"Jennifer. Is my brother in?"

"Yes, he is. Um, are you going to your office?"

The girl glanced on down the hall to Elizabeth's right and then at Rand. She had the funniest look on her face, as though she was embarrassed to look at him. Her eyes kept darting away. Elizabeth was used to this. Most people didn't know how to react to a blind person. At least Jennifer wasn't yelling as if Rand was deaf.

"No. I've come to see Max. Is he available?"

"Yes. There's no one else here right now. He's on the phone with the Colorado office."

"Thank you, Jennifer."

Jennifer went past them into a room to the left.

"She was acting like I had leprosy, wasn't she?"

Rand's voice was tinged with bitterness.

"She wasn't *that* bad," Elizabeth said, turning left and going down the hall. "Actually, I think if you decide to come back to work here, Jennifer is going to be an asset to you."

Rand didn't comment. They continued down the long hall until they came to a door with a gold nameplate on it. "Max is on one end and I'm on the other," Rand explained as if realizing she was wondering why his name wasn't up there. "He's in charge of the financial end of things while I work with the rest."

"Chief financial officer."

Rand smiled. "You could say that. He used to tease me and say that sounded so trivial when we were talking billions of dollars."

"Wow!" Elizabeth said again, suitably impressed.

They opened the door and she looked around the large secretarial office. "I would never have guessed a man's office would be decorated in mauves and pinks and browns. Well, maybe browns. Oh, my," she said, looking to the left. "That painting, is it an original?"

She started that way, but Rand held tight. "Yes, it is, and you're not leaving me alone until I'm seated in Max's office."

Recalling herself she turned toward the oak door. "Just go on in," he said, and Elizabeth obeyed.

At the sound of the door, Max turned. He was still on the phone. His gaze met hers and she noticed how tired he looked. "Uh, I'll call you back," he immediately said. "Just go with what you're doing. I'll get a date to fly out there."

As soon as the phone hit the cradle Max was striding around the desk. "Rand! It's great to see you. I didn't know you were coming."

Rand felt for a chair and then seated himself. Elizabeth could easily picture him on the other side of the large mahogany desk. She glanced across the opulent room to where a leather couch and chairs were arranged around a fireplace.

She never dreamed offices had fireplaces.

"For soothing purposes only. It's not real."

"Huh?"

Max grinned. "You were staring at the fireplace."

"Why don't we all go over there?" Max asked. "Can I get you something to drink?" He went to the bar as Rand stood. He pulled out a diet drink and clinked ice cubes into a glass. Elizabeth nodded agreement. He poured both of them the same thing then got Rand tea.

"Orange tea, Rand," Max said, coming to the sofa where Rand had seated himself. When Elizabeth started to move off, Rand gave her a little jerk, causing her to fall back on the couch by him.

Max raised an eyebrow at her as he handed the tea to Rand.

She flushed and tried to put a little room between them on the white couch. But the leather was so plush that his weight kept her close. She decided to ignore the looks Max cast her and sip her drink.

"So, what brings you out? Not that I'm not glad. I wish you were back here already."

Rand frowned. "You know that's impossible, Max."

Max opened his mouth but Elizabeth gave a little shake of her head. Rand was definitely not ready to talk about returning to the office. He had stiffened up like a fireplace poker when she had mentioned it in the hallway.

"We went to lunch," Elizabeth said. She saw the flash of hurt in Max's eyes and realized he would have wanted to come along. "Next time you're going to have to come with us," she added, smiling.

"What was that about going to Colorado?" Rand asked.

"Jackson thinks we've got an embezzler in the district office. He has an idea who it is. I told him I'd fly out and go over all the information before anything was done."

"That's not necessary."

"It is when he's accusing a man who has been with us for over thirty years."

"Ah. So when are you leaving?"

"In a few days, maybe a week. I have things that need catching up on here. The man won't be going anywhere. He has no idea Jackson has stumbled onto any problems."

Rand nodded. "Actually, while I was here, I wondered if you might update me on some of the business. I just can't stand the thought of going back to the house on a Saturday and sitting around all day."

Elizabeth couldn't, either. The tension between Rand and herself was enough to drive a sane person to commit a crazy act, like possibly kissing the perpetrator of that tension. And she didn't consider herself sane at the moment—otherwise she wouldn't be thinking about a patient in such terms.

"I'd be happy to give you an update, Rand. And I have some problems I need to ask you about, if you don't mind."

Rand replied with a casual shrug. But Elizabeth knew better. Rand was truly excited. This was the first time she'd seen him show a real interest in his work. "I'll just sit here and read, if you don't mind."

"You brought a book?" Rand asked.

She chuckled. "No. But there are magazines. And if I get bored, this couch looks real comfortable."

Max laughed and turned his attention to Rand, totally dismissing Elizabeth from his mind.

Elizabeth didn't mind. When Rand stood and turned toward her for help, she looked at Max.

"Uh, show me what to do," he said to Rand. "I can help."

Rand hesitated then took Max's elbow.

Elizabeth smiled. Today couldn't have turned out better than if she had planned it herself.

Yes, today was going to go down as one of the best days in the entire time they'd been working together.

Chapter Ten

~❧~

It was one of the worst days of Elizabeth's life.

She now understood the phrase *media frenzy*.

None of them had realized the media had gotten pictures of her and Rand at Mama Ria's. Nor had they realized several reporters had followed them and were waiting at the main door for them to exit.

Of course, Rand wouldn't have used that door if Max hadn't insisted he and Rand show Elizabeth the entire building.

Because of the tour, Rand had the car brought around front.

As soon as she and Rand exited out the front door, people descended on them. Rand was knocked away from her. "Mr. Stevens! Mr. Stevens!" reporters began yelling. "Is it true your brother, Rand, has someone living at the house with him?"

Elizabeth saw Rand fighting his way through the crowd, but he was heading in the wrong direction. She pushed and shoved, not caring what people thought, as she battled her way to him.

When she got to his side, she reached for him, only to be pushed away. "Rand!" she called, and immediately realized her mistake. One of the reporters heard her. "Rand Stevens?"

Luckily, he was the only one who heard her besides Rand. His arms reached out and wrapped around her. With determined strides she started forward, pushing and shoving, getting jostled and even cussed out as she made her way to the car. The driver, seeing what was happening, had a path cleared in only moments.

But they were some of the worst moments of her life—shoving, cursing, flashes going off, microphones being shoved into their faces. Someone even asked about the embezzlement situation. So much for no one knowing about the problem in Colorado.

They fell into the car. The door was slammed behind them and then the driver jumped in and drove off.

"Are you okay?" Elizabeth asked Rand.

She could feel his trembling. "I'm so sorry I let you get separated. I didn't realize those people were reporters."

"I guess they knew Max was inside working from seeing the car out front." He picked up the phone and dialed Max's number. "The word is out about the embezzlement, Max," he said as soon as Max picked up. "We were just mobbed by reporters."

Rand listened then said bitterly, "Yes, I'm fine. Just helpless as a newborn babe."

There was a pause, then, "Now you see why I'll never be any help outside the house."

Elizabeth sighed as Rand hung up the phone.

"Maybe in time," she began.

"Don't. I won't *ever* go through that again."

She reached for his hand. "Maybe—"

"You don't know what it was like. Hands grabbing me, being pushed every which way and unable to do a single thing about it. All I could think of was what if they propelled me into the street where the cars were zooming past. I could hear them going by and just knew I was going to end up in front of one of them."

"I would have never let that happen."

"But you won't always be there, will you?"

She couldn't argue with that. "You can have the driver wait at the door to escort you. There are many ways around that—"

"Forget it. I just want to go home."

Elizabeth nodded, squeezed Rand's hand and started to release it, only to find that he wouldn't free her hand. They rode together in silence until they reached the house.

Rand, exhausted, went in and dressed in his swimsuit. He did a few laps and then retired to his rooms, telling Elizabeth he wanted to rest.

Elizabeth agreed. She needed rest, too. They decided to meet downstairs in the den before dinner.

Elizabeth walked into the den, her soft multicolored skirt and sleeveless top with its starched collar feeling cool in the air-conditioned room. She had debated on dressing so relaxed and feminine, but decided since it was a meal there would be no harm. Besides, tonight she wanted to feel pretty and soft and feminine. Rand couldn't see her, and she insisted it wasn't for Rand that she was wearing the outfit, not at all. She just liked to dress all soft and flowing occasionally.

"Better come look at this," Max said, staring intently at the television. Rand was seated next to him.

"What?" she questioned, walking over to the arm of the couch, near Rand but not too near.

"Evidently today there was a news camera there as well as photographers. Seems they got pictures of us."

Rand's voice was hard and angry.

Elizabeth's stomach sank. She hadn't thought of being on television. After talking with Rand last night, she'd felt better than she had felt in ages, so good, in fact, that she forgot about the threat always looming just over her horizon.

She sank down next to Rand. Max glanced at her and then his brother, but only briefly. A commercial ended and the TV reporter's face reappeared.

"As we were saying earlier," the smiling reporter said to the camera, "the Stevens brothers are always full of news. And today was no exception. Our local reporter was downtown to investigate the alleged embezzlement investigation that is currently ongoing at one of the regional offices. However, when we arrived, instead of finding that, well, why don't we just let you watch this?"

The picture cut to Rand and Elizabeth exiting the building and being surrounded by reporters. Elizabeth gasped.

"What?" Rand demanded.

"We're coming out of the office and then you were pulled away. I... Oh, no..." she moaned.

"What?"

"You have a good right hook, Elizabeth," Max said, his eyes widening. "Evidently, big brother, your therapist didn't appreciate being separated from— Oh, this is good. She not only punched out a photographer but knocked him down, and if I'm not mistaken, she stepped on one of those gentlemen who was shoving a microphone in her face. What was evidently a frenzy has turned into a brawl.''

You could hear the shouts and an occasional cry of pain. ''The reporters are shoving each other to get closer. Ah, they heard the name Rand.''

It ended and the reporter's face reappeared. ''Was that the recluse, Rand Stevens, or his brother, Max, who has been holding down the business since the tragedy over a year ago? And who was the woman? My guess, a bodyguard. It is rumored that a contract was taken out on Max's life after discovering the embezzlement and—''

Max clicked the TV off.

''Good heavens,'' Elizabeth whispered. ''A contract?''

Max looked at her, nudged Rand then burst out laughing. ''Well, that's the first time I've had a contract out on me.''

''How'd they get the information?'' Rand demanded.

''You've been gone too long, brother. You know the way gossip works. I've had someone tracing the possible embezzlement for over two weeks. It finally reached the wrong ears.''

''Or right ears. Find out who leaked it.''

''Yeah, right.''

Elizabeth listened to them argue. But all she could think of was that once again her face had been on TV.

''Elizabeth?'' Max called.

She didn't realize she was gripping Rand's hand until she felt him squeeze in return. ''Yes?'' she said, pulling her hand away, and missing the warmth.

''I asked if you were okay. You didn't handle it very well last time you saw yourself on TV and you're pale as a ghost now.''

"I'm fine. Really," she reassured him.

Rand's brow furrowed as if he knew she was lying. She cleared her throat. "Really. It's no big deal." She stood. "If that's over, can we go to dinner now? I'm famished."

No one argued. They all stood and went in to dine. Rand found it increasingly easy to eat his meals with Max and Elizabeth. It was still humiliating when he spilled something, but not quite as bad as it had been the first time. Tonight they had baked cod in a light butter sauce with asparagus and new potatoes.

The meal passed with little conversation from Elizabeth, and all too soon she was done. "Do you mind if I go on up?" she asked Rand. "I'm rather tired tonight."

"Not at all," he said.

He heard her rise, bid her good-night and listened to the slight swish of her skirt as she left the dining room. When she was gone Max cleared his throat. "What's bothering her?"

"You noticed?" Rand asked, surprised. "What gave her away?"

"Her face. She kept drifting off, her eyes taking on a hazy look as if she were a million miles away."

"Or maybe just a few hundred."

"What do you mean by that?" Max asked. The scrape of his plate indicated he had pushed it away. Rand did the same.

He leaned back in his chair, his hands across his abdomen, flat from all the working out he'd been doing lately. He had certainly filled out since Elizabeth had been here. "It has to do with last night."

"Last night?"

Rand heard wariness in Max's voice. "You know better than that, Max."

"Hey, after two separate nurses tried to further their friendship..."

"Elizabeth's not like that!"

"I didn't think so," Max said lightly.

Rand scowled. "I—well, I thought she had gone out on a date and waited in her room, only intending to talk to her. Instead, I surprised her."

When Rand paused, trying to think how to explain, Max asked, "Surprised her? How?"

"I was sitting there, on the sofa. I guess she didn't see me. I thought she intended to walk right past me because she was miffed from earlier in the day. I reached out and snagged her hand."

"And?" Max prompted.

"She came apart. Went crazy. Started fighting me. I thought she was going to scratch my eyes out, until I heard her call me Michael."

"Michael? Her date?"

"She didn't have a date. Michael is her ex-fiancé."

"Ah, I see," Max said. "No, well, no, I don't see."

"She evidently had a jerk of a fiancé who...abused her." The last was a whisper. Every time Rand thought of that his blood boiled anew. She was so tiny and fragile.

"You're kidding."

Rand didn't answer.

A loud sigh came from Max. "You hear about it but just never expect it to be someone you know."

"I just thought maybe seeing the news program...you said she was fighting them, hitting, and I remember most of the voices were male... I thought maybe she was remembering her ex-fiancé."

"Is he still around?"

Rand frowned. "I don't know. I don't even think Eliz abeth is from this area. She's moved around a lot."

"But you still think this is about her ex?"

"She has a lot of unresolved fear, as I can attest to, and guilt."

"Guilt?"

"She received some internal damage. She can't have children. I think she blames herself for not breaking it off sooner." Rand leaned forward, his face strained with the memories of last night. "Max, you should have seen her. My heart broke. I wanted to go out and kill the man who had put her through all of that. She's afraid it'll get around here. That's why she was so reluctant to tell me everything. She said she's happy here. I'm glad for her and don't want her hurt again."

"It goes without saying, brother. We both know what it's like to be considered different."

"But she's not different, Max. She's funny, always cracking these awful jokes. She loves doing daredevil stunts, is accident-prone, always has been. Just because this happened in her past is no reason for anyone to treat her like a leper."

"I see."

His cheery voice sounded at odds with the subject. Rand frowned. "See what?"

"Nothing, Rand. Look, I've got to put in a call to Colorado. Why don't you go up and find out if that's what's bothering Elizabeth. She might just need some-one to talk to. Even if she doesn't want to talk it wouldn't hurt to let her know we're concerned about her."

Rand nodded. "Maybe you're right." He stood. Max and Rand walked to the door together. Just as they reached it the phone rang. Max picked it up. "Hello?"

Rand started toward the stairs.

"Hello?"

He heard a click. "A hang-up call. I was expecting a reporter."

Rand chuckled. "As long as *you* deal with them. I have had it with those reporters. Hey, speaking of which, would you call the station and mention our displeasure at the disclosure of such speculation?"

"Sure. I'm certain they'll be thrilled to hear from one of us personally. As a matter of fact, I'll promise them an interview when I get back from Colorado if they leave us alone in the meantime."

Rand shook his head. He didn't know how Max did it. He would personally like to go out and slap a slander suit or something on those people for upsetting Elizabeth. Max, on the other hand, just smiled, dealt with any calls to the house and blew it off.

Rand knocked at Elizabeth's door, waiting patiently until she answered it.

It was immediately evident from the humidity surrounding her and the fresh smell of soap what she had been doing. "Did I interrupt you?"

"Not at all. Come on in." She escorted him into the room and took a seat in one of the chairs near the balcony doors. "As it's so cool out this evening I opened the doors to let in some fresh air. Care to join me?"

He went to the other chair near the doors and seated himself.

"The evenings are so beautiful, peaceful, although rather humid," she joked.

"Max seems to think you were upset during dinner."

Elizabeth was quiet for a minute. "And you?" she finally asked.

"You didn't eat anything, only toyed with your food."

She sighed.

"What is it, Elizabeth?"

"Nothing. I just... Well, for several years after Michael and I broke up, he stalked me. A few years ago he broke the injunction and was arrested. He was put in jail for six months. That's when I moved here. I can't help but worry that one day he's going to find me."

"You think he's still looking?"

"I don't know."

Rand leaned back in his chair and crossed his ankles. "I would imagine jail woke him up. Just how long have you lived here now?"

"Three years. I moved right after he went to jail."

"Three years." Rand considered. "That's an awfully long time. If you want, though, I can hire a private investigator and have him find out just where Michael is."

He heard her quickly indrawn breath. "But why? There's no need—"

"There's every need, Elizabeth," he said before she could say that he was only her patient. That line had irritated him to no end. "No woman should have to live in constant fear. Let me hire a detective and find out where the man is now and what he's doing."

"I don't know," Elizabeth said, hedging.

"As a friend, Elizabeth. Nothing else. Besides," he said, standing, "if you don't let me do it, I'll just do it without your permission. It might take longer, but I'll still find out."

"You're a very stubborn man, Rand Stevens."

"And you're not a stubborn woman?"

"Touché," she said, and chuckled.

"Good night. See you at six in the morning."

"That's right. And Rand?"

He paused at her door. "Yes?"

"We're going to learn basic office management over the next few days. I hope you're ready."

"I'm ready for whatever you can dish out, my Elizabeth. Whatever you can dish out."

Chapter Eleven

"Why did the dinosaur cross the road?"

Rand groaned.

"Hey, it's not a chicken joke," Elizabeth said, sailing into the main room of his suite. "Well," she said, "not exactly."

"I don't know. Why *did* the dinosaur cross the road?" he asked, as if it put him out to ask it.

"Because there were no chickens back then!" she said then burst into giggles.

Rand couldn't help it, he smiled. "You're certainly in a good mood this morning."

"I am ready to get to work. You've eaten, I know, I checked with Sarah. And I've eaten. The sun is up. It's cool outside and we're *finally* going to get to do something I love to do."

"What's that?" he asked, going toward her voice.

"Work on a computer."

Rand reached out until he found her hair. Lowering his hand to her shoulder, he felt the soft cotton fabric. "Tell me what you're wearing today?" he asked.

She hesitated.

"Come on," he cajoled, feeling extremely easygoing this morning after a good night's sleep. It was the first night he'd gone without a nightmare. "*You* can see my tan slacks and yellow pullover shirt. At least clue me in."

"Well," she said, drawing the word out. "I have a pale green shirt on. It's cotton, button up, tiny flat buttons—white. And believe it or not, a skirt."

"Green, too?" he asked, picturing the short woman with red hair in green. He'd seen women with red hair. Green usually complemented their coloring.

"No. It's multicolored. The small print is primarily forest green, but it has browns and yellows and oranges with it. Muted orange," she added.

Orange? "Are you a tanned redhead or a freckled redhead?" he asked, and felt her stiffen. "Sorry, I shouldn't have asked that." He backed up.

"That's okay. I'm tanned, but I have freckles across my nose, if you *must* know." Her voice was light. He was glad he hadn't offended her.

"Done asking questions?"

"I suppose, for now," he said, just to let her know she wasn't completely off the hook. "I was simply curious."

"I understand," she said, heading toward the door.

He wondered if she really did. She was driving him nuts. She had on a different perfume today. It was musky, reminding him of candle-lit dinners.

She opened the door to his office and he followed her in. It was the first time he'd been in here since she had added some special equipment. "Come on over to the desk. I haven't moved anything, except I've added things to your computer."

"Am I going to think I'm in the world of Star Trek when I sit here?" he asked, referring to the many trips she'd made bringing in the new equipment.

She only chuckled.

When he was seated, she handed him a stack of papers. "I want you to go through this mail for the last three days. I know someone else usually does this, but you never know when you might be here alone and you want to find something. You can identify the most important mail by the size of the envelope. Any oversize envelopes or undersize pieces of paper will go into one pile. All the regular size envelopes—the more important mail—will go in another pile."

She stopped talking and pulled a chair up next to him. He hated doing mundane things like this. This was when he would feel the most foolish if he made a mistake. One by one he sorted the letters into two piles. When he was done, he asked, "Did I do that right?"

She sighed. "There is no right or wrong, Rand. This is simply a learning process. As I said, you will probably hire a secretary to help you with any sorting or paperwork, so this isn't any big deal. It's just a way to familiarize yourself with common tasks."

She took his hand and moved it from his lap to the desk. "Find the index cards and get two. You want to write today's date with one of the Hi Mark pens and then affix it with a rubber band to the top of each pile."

He fumbled until he found the special pen and the cards. In amazingly quick order he was done.

"There are two stacked files here for each group of mail. However, since we want to work with the important mail, you will leave that one out."

"Now what?" he asked, wondering how in the world she expected him to do this every day.

"In front of your keyboard is a scanner. Open the first letter and slip it into the scanner. The scanner will read you the mail and convert it into a text file if you want. If you don't, you simply push *n* at the end of the message and the computer will delete the information from its memory."

They spent the next hour learning how to operate the personal reader. Then Elizabeth pulled out templates for the checks she'd had Max get for Rand. She showed him how easy it was to lay the template over the check, fill out the date and amount and then add his signature.

"I can't believe this," he finally said. "I never knew any of this special equipment even existed."

"That's because you didn't need it."

He was impressed.

"It won't make you one hundred percent self-sufficient, but it will give you a large part of your life back. You'll be able to fill out your own checks now, keep your own files, if you have any desire to do such a disgusting duty, and even read your mail in the privacy of your own house. Later, as you learn some basic Braille, you will be able to read when you're out on your own."

"I don't want to talk about that," he said, her enthusiasm about going out ruining his mood. Despite what she said, he knew he would never go out by himself. He was blind, and there was no use trying to do things that might endanger him or someone else. No, he would be perfectly happy here, or with someone when he was out.

"I knew a person once who owned his own business. He found, with his wife's help and an assistant, he could keep the business open. I'm sure Max would appreciate your help, even if it's from the house. And with on-line services now you can do all kinds of things from this room.''

She sighed, and he realized they had been working for some time. "Talking computer, talking clock on the computer...it's unbelievable what you've done." And she hadn't changed anything around on his desk. He didn't necessarily remember where everything was, but as he touched each object, more and more was coming back to him.

He closed his files with only a little difficulty and turned to Elizabeth. "Can we go for a walk? My mind is fuzzy after so many hours on the computer."

She agreed.

He went to the balcony doors and opened them. "It's after lunch," he said, suddenly realizing he was hungry. "Maybe we should send word to Sarah to have lunch out on the patio ready in about half an hour."

"Sounds good," she said, but he couldn't tell what she was feeling. "Be right back," she called, then hurried out the door. In seconds she was back.

"Well," she said as they started down the stairs. "Did you learn much this morning?"

He smiled. "How much you enjoy computers," he said.

She laughed and he was enchanted. Soft, musical, her voice had the ability to get rid of the stress clutching at his shoulders. "What perfume do you have on?" he asked, catching another whiff of the spicy scent.

"Midnight," she replied. "Why?"

"I miss the citrusy one. It was more wild, more free."

"Wild?" she asked, laughing again.

"Okay, just, well, like a lemon tree or orange orchard. How's that?"

"Better. I'm not wild, by any means."

"Remember, you've told me about all the bones you've broken on your escapades."

"Oh, I did, didn't I?" He wished he could see her eyes. He was almost certain she was flirting with him.

"Let's walk through the garden," he said.

She promptly turned in that direction.

"I enjoy walking out here in the evenings after dinner. I haven't been out here in a long time, though."

Elizabeth was surprised. "All you had to do was tell me and I would come with you."

"I wasn't ready to share it with anyone," he said, and she wasn't sure what he meant until they rounded the corner.

"What do you do with your evenings, Elizabeth? The first week or so you spent them with me, nagging me constantly," he said, only half joking. "But now, I rarely see you."

She smiled. "You need time alone, Rand. If you get lonely or want to talk, I'm only across the hall."

"That's not why I was asking," he said, reaching down and entwining his hand with hers as they walked. "I was just curious."

Elizabeth's heart was doing double time from the moment he had taken her hand. She wasn't sure what to do. Pull away? Tell him he was her patient? Or give in and enjoy what she had so badly wanted for the past few days, just to be with him as a man and a woman who enjoyed each other's company? She decided on the latter. Ever since the night of her confession things had changed. He was easier around her, willing to listen, learn, try new things. And she was able to talk, open up and share as she had never been able to before.

So why was she having a problem with enjoying their time together?

Because she knew she was going to be leaving. He was the first man who could touch her heart in some mysterious way, and she would soon be going on to another patient, soon to be forgotten by this one. She'd been here over two months, and should have already left, but Max had encouraged her to stay just a little longer. And as there was no immediate need for her else-where…

"I usually read," she said, refusing to continue her line of thought. Leaving would come soon enough. She decided to enjoy the here and now.

"You enjoy reading?"

"Yes."

"I never did. I was always too busy doing something else. I knew one day I'd have time to sit down and read but later, when I had time…"

"You still can," she said softly, seeing the wistful look in his eyes.

"I know." He sighed. "Tell me what's blooming," he said as he pushed the gate open and they passed under the arch at the entrance to a private, walled-in garden.

"Why don't you tell me?" she countered.

"Because I like to hear you talk."

She flushed. Her heart fluttered, then she gave in. "It's really very beautiful. Hydrangeas, blue and pink, are re-ally blooming well. There are some orange blooms—"

"Trumpeter vines."

"Yes. They're just starting to open up. Let's see, roses, only a few, yellow, red, orange and, oh, how pretty, pink. I am a pink fan myself, though it doesn't go real good with my skin and hair color."

He chuckled. "I bet that doesn't stop you."

"Why, no," she said, effecting a Southern drawl, "it doesn't, dahlin'."

He smiled. "What else?"

"Pink and red azaleas line the wall. It's a veritable jungle in here."

"There are all types of blooming flowers, enough that there is something blooming just about year round. Right now, though, in the spring, is my favorite time to be in here. Take the right path," he said as they approached a fork.

She did as he bid. "Why this way? Something else you want me to see?"

He grinned. "Oh, yeah," he murmured and she heated up at the sexy drawl in his voice.

They rounded another curve, and a small fountain came into view. It was so typical, a woman holding a vase with water drizzling out. In front of it was a bench. However typical the setting, Elizabeth thought it was beautiful just the same. She led him toward the bench. "I take it the fountain was the surprise up this path?"

He pulled her down beside him. The sound of the bubbling water, mixed with the swaying of the magnolia and dogwood trees, gave off a sense of peace. "Not exactly," he murmured. "We've been closed up in the house all day, people going up and down the halls cleaning. The gardeners were mowing and working in the gardens in the front of the house. This was the only place I could think of to be alone without someone watching."

Thinking he was feeling insecure again, she said, "None of your staff stare at you. There's no reason to avoid them."

"Oh, but they would stare, believe me."

"Why?" she asked, having no idea what he was talking about.

"They'd stare because they would think it was unusual, maybe even shocking, to see their boss kiss his therapist.''

Elizabeth's eyes widened and she started to lean back, but she was too late. Rand lowered his head and nuzzled her neck. "I've been wanting to do this all morning. However, I knew you'd have a fit if I even tried it while we were working."

"And what makes you think I won't throw a fit now?" she asked breathlessly.

"Because you want this just as much as I do."

She couldn't lie. His lips trailed up her jaw, over her eyes and finally settled on her lips.

A soft sigh escaped her as she melted into him and allowed him to kiss her the way he wanted. It was sweet, gentle, caring, giving as well as taking. And when he was done, Elizabeth didn't pull back but laid her head against his shoulder. "This won't work," she whispered even as she clung to him trying to absorb his strength. "I'm scarred and battle weary from my past and you haven't let go of your grief."

"Your scars will heal."

"And you?" Elizabeth asked, pain lacing her words. "Will you ever be able to let go of the pain and guilt, to live again? Will you ever be able to go to church and not blame yourself or God?"

"Stop it," Rand warned, leaning back. "You don't understand. I can't go to church and…"

"And?" she asked, hopeful that he was finally going to open up about what was bothering him.

"Nothing. I don't blame God, exactly. But—" he stood and took a couple of steps away from her "—I can't take that responsibility for someone again. I was fully functional then, always in control, but it was a facade. It cost my wife her life. You can't understand that.

To take that chance again when I'm blind, like I am…
It would be too much of a risk to ask someone to share
that. And I wouldn't ask them because I don't want that
responsibility.''

Elizabeth went to him and touched his shoulder, but
he shrugged her away, obviously still upset.

''You'll have to forgive yourself sooner or later and
let someone inside your shell. If you would let God in,
let Him get rid of the burden you're carrying, you might
find that you'd be able to step out and risk heartache
again. There's always chance with everything you do,
but that doesn't mean you have to stop living.''

''You can't know what I'm talking about,'' he said,
anger in his voice.

''But I do. If you'll remember, I lost more than just
a fiancé—I lost the ability to give life to a new soul.''

''And have you started living again? Or are you simply hiding behind God, using Him as a barrier from
everyone else?''

Elizabeth fell back in shock and hurt. She had never
thought about the way she held on to God as a barrier,
but looking back on her prayers, she realized how many
times she had told God that He was all she needed and
to please not send any men her way.

But for Rand to be so callous… ''I live,'' she whispered.

''But will you ever risk marriage? You just said you
were battered and bruised from your past. Yet you expect me to go to church, smile and act like nothing has
happened. I cannot go to church, face God, tell Him
what I'm feeling. I can't do it!''

Elizabeth swallowed her pain. ''You're going to have
to, Rand. You're only going to be able to go so far
before you have to face it.''

Even as she said it, she realized she was being brought to that crossroads herself. One by one since she had been here, at Rand's mansion, her old hurts and pains had been dredged up—by accident or design, she wondered—and brought out in the open. "I know what I'm talking about. You're going to have to face them or totally close yourself off."

"What do you want me to do? Confess how miserable I am? Okay, I am! I want to live again, but not if it means risking someone else's well-being. I'm blind now. I couldn't protect Carolyn when she was alive. How can I protect anyone else?"

There was the crux of his problem. "I don't know," she answered truthfully. "That's got to be between you and God. But think about this. Did you do everything you could have to keep Carolyn safe? Did you try? Don't second-guess your decisions. You'll never know if it would've been better to stay at home. How do you know she wouldn't have been killed the next day? You don't know. Believe me, I've second-guessed enough to know how little it helps and how much it hurts."

She turned from him, looking out over the garden, knowing he was even now thinking about his wife as his tormented eyes stared sightlessly into the distance. "Until you reach out and live again, and that includes taking chances and risks, you'll never truly be free."

"Go on to the house," he said, rubbing his forehead as if in pain. "Ask Sarah to send someone else out here to walk me back."

Elizabeth's shoulders slumped. He was angry. He didn't want to be around her. She turned to go. "Max and I are going to church tomorrow night. If you change your mind, we'd be glad if you went with us."

He didn't answer, only turned his back to her and sat on the bench.

Oh, well, she thought. She'd made them both miserable, but something good had come of it. He now knew why it wouldn't work between them. He wanted her, but not enough to let go of the past and offer marriage. And she would settle for nothing less. She was not going to give her heart to a man who could not love her back.

Father, God, please tell me that this pain will quickly pass, she thought, leaving the garden. *Tell me that all of the past about my ex-fiancé is gone and that this revaluation was the only reason you sent me here. I'll no longer hurt. I won't give my heart to that man. And he'll heal in time, with someone else leading him through the rest of his valley.*

There was no answer, just the distant chirping of birds.

But Elizabeth didn't need an answer because she knew God wasn't done with her yet. The tormented look in Rand's eyes would be there for a long time, and she wouldn't be happy until she saw it gone.

Chapter Twelve

Elizabeth parked her car in the usual spot. It was dark, and she was just coming home from church—alone. Max had ended up leaving earlier than expected for Colorado. In a way she was glad she had been alone. Max and Rand attracted too much media attention for her comfort.

But the other problem with being alone was that she had to go inside and up the stairs where Rand was probably waiting for her.

Rand hadn't mentioned what had happened between them yesterday, going on as if nothing unusual had been discussed. But Elizabeth could see the misery in his eyes. She wanted to shake him, tell him it was okay to be afraid, that if he would just turn to God, he would be released from that fear.

But she knew she couldn't, because until yesterday she hadn't realized how she had allowed her fears of her ex-fiancé to shape her life.

She was afraid to care for Rand because she knew something bad was going to happen again. How ridiculous that sounded. Yet that was how she felt. She realized she needed to confront her past, deal with it and go forward instead of dragging her pains and fears along with her like some cumbersome piece of baggage.

And so did Rand.

But she was at a loss on how to help him open up again and accept that life had risks. ''Father, please help him,'' she whispered, swinging open her car door. ''Because I don't know how.''

She closed the door and decided to go up the balcony steps. She'd left her doors open earlier. She often came in that way instead of through the kitchen door. She rarely used the main door—the foyer was too intimidating. She rounded the corner of the house and slowed her step.

Looking toward Rand's window, which was on this side of the mansion, she wondered if she ought to check on him just to make sure he was okay, then decided the distance between them was good. She shouldn't ruin that.

While she was standing there debating with herself, a shadow detached itself from the wall and crept toward the balcony stairs.

Elizabeth started to step forward, but the way the shadow moved stopped her. Something wasn't right. She watched the shadow and suddenly realized what it was that was bothering her. One of the staff wouldn't sneak up the stairs like this shadow was doing.

Heart beating a staccato rhythm, Elizabeth whirled and ran as quietly as possible to the kitchen entrance. Trembling, she almost dropped her key before finally getting in the door. Dropping her purse and kicking off her heels, she sprinted toward the staircase. ''Rand!'' she called quietly, doing her best not to alert the intruder.

She pushed his door open and ran into his room.

"Rand!" she whispered frantically, running toward his bed. She reach out, searching. "Rand!"

A hand clamped over her wrist. "What? What's the matter?"

"There's an intruder outside." She glanced toward the balcony doors. "Oh, dear heavens," she said, leaning forward until her lips were against his ear, "I see a shadow."

He swung his feet over the edge of the bed. "Did you call the police?" he asked as he crept into the main part of the suite.

Before she answered, they heard the rattle of the door. It was locked. "I haven't opened it since the maid cleaned this morning," he said by way of explanation even as he picked up the phone and dialed the police.

Immediately his call was answered and Rand explained the situation.

"Did you lock the door downstairs when you came in?" he asked, hanging up the portable in its cradle.

Elizabeth simply stared, not believing her stupidity.

"Did you?" he asked, gripping her.

"No."

He complained under his breath. "Well, it's too late. You're not going down there, and I sure can't do anything. Let's go to the bathroom and lock ourselves in."

"But the intruder. What if he gets in?"

"Like I said, what can I do? And I'm not letting you wander this house unprotected."

Oh, dear. She heard the bitterness in his voice. "Well, you couldn't do anything if you could see, either," she said, even as he propelled her into the bathroom. "After all, it's dangerous to face a criminal. That's what the police are for."

Without a word he shoved her into the bathroom and

locked the door behind him. "I'd rather not discuss this or we're just going to end up on the same conversation as yesterday. This is just more proof about what I said. If you ever got into real trouble I wouldn't be able to help you."

"I didn't ask you to protect me."

"But if we were married you would."

"Married?" she squeaked.

He let out a loud sigh. "Don't mind me, I must be crazy. I have no idea what I'm saying."

Elizabeth wholeheartedly agreed. After all, she and Rand were just attracted to each other, that was all, wasn't it?

"Listen, Elizabeth…"

Just then they heard Rand's name being called. He unlocked the door and they stepped out of the bathroom. In the hallway they were met by a police officer. "I came on in when you didn't immediately answer, Mr. Stevens."

"That's quite all right. Did you find the person?"

"We certainly did. Local rag magazine wanted to get the scoop on you. He was evidently trying to find your room."

"A reporter," Rand said flatly.

"Yeah, don't that beat all? Guess living the life of the privileged does have some drawbacks. You can give us your report and then we'll leave you alone."

Elizabeth smiled at the police officer. "If you don't mind, I'll go on to my room."

"We'll need to know what you saw first, ma'am."

She quickly told him, looked at Rand, who had seated himself on the couch, and said, "Do you need anything else, Rand?"

"No. Go on. I'll see Timms locks up when everyone's gone."

"The butler?" the police officer asked. "I'd like to ask him about your alarm system. Seems like it's only wired to the lower doors."

"That's right. It was put in years ago but I never got around to wiring the balcony doors I had put in when I had the house renovated a few years back. But you can talk to him. I'm sure he'll be able to tell you exactly what is wired and what isn't."

Elizabeth escaped while they were still talking.

She wasn't sure what Rand had been planning to say before the policeman had interrupted him, and she wasn't sure she wanted to know. She had blown it again with him. She needed to learn to keep her mouth shut. He was going to believe what he wanted and there was nothing she could do about it.

But he was hurting so bad. On a physical level he had learned almost all she could teach him. In a few weeks he'd be ready to go out. Hadn't he already started displaying an impatience to get out? But his emotions... She hated to leave someone she was afraid would be scarred for a long time if she couldn't get him to face his problems.

I know, she thought, looking at herself in the mirror. *Oh, how I know. But it isn't up to me to heal him.*

She quickly undressed and crawled in bed. She closed her eyes and prayed, hoping that she would find the solace she needed in the arms of the One who cared for her.

Rand felt like a grouch.

Elizabeth had come upstairs to warn him and all he could do was gripe at her.

He knew it wasn't her he was angry at, but at his blindness. Just when he thought he was learning to function again he had to face something like this. He turned onto his back and stared sightlessly at the canopy over his bed.

What he couldn't understand was why Elizabeth couldn't see what he could. He was not ever going to be normal again. He couldn't protect her. His wife had lost her life when he was in control of his own life. But now, blind, how could he help Elizabeth if something happened?

He stacked his hands behind his head.

Still, that didn't give him the right to take out his anger on her. She was doing her best to help him learn to function as well as possible. Of course it was her job to be a Pollyanna, to encourage him to do things he knew were impossible.

But she wasn't happy with just his physical well-being. She wanted him to be whole in every way, just like he had been before the accident. And even if he did talk to God about what was going on, he knew that wasn't going to fill that gaping, empty whole inside him. It was only going to make him more miserable because he would never forgive himself for not trying harder.

And as much as he was attracted to Elizabeth, he would carry the attraction no further because he would not take on the responsibility of someone else and then risk not being able to protect them when they needed him.

If he couldn't do it when he could see, he sure couldn't do it now.

Elizabeth didn't understand that.

But she would.

Still, he should probably apologize to her for being such a jerk.

Could he do that and keep his distance? She said she only had a few more weeks, at most. Would he be able to hide the feelings he was developing for her that long?

A sound disturbed his thoughts.

He pulled his hands from behind his head and pushed up in the bed, listening.

The intruder had unnerved him. It was something else to know someone was right outside your door and not be able to see him. All kinds of scenarios had run through his head before the police got there.

That was one reason he was having so much trouble going to sleep.

That and Elizabeth.

He touched his bedside clock. Four in the morning.

He heard a sound like a squeak or cry, far off—or muffled? It hadn't sounded like an intruder, but some-one...crying.

Elizabeth?

Rand slid from his bed and made his way through his suite. He padded barefoot to Elizabeth's door, where he paused and listened.

Nothing.

He waited another minute but when he didn't hear anything he turned to go.

A cry rent the air.

Rand whirled. He pushed open Elizabeth's door and made his way to her room. "Elizabeth?" he called out. Her whimpers were clear now.

She didn't answer, and he realized she must be having a dream. "Elizabeth?" he said again, softly, inching his way carefully across her bedroom floor, his hands out in front of him.

She still didn't answer.

He sank down on the edge of the bed and tentatively felt around until he encountered flesh. It was her arm.

He shook it cautiously before sliding his hand down to her hand and clasping it firmly between his own. "Come on, honey, wake up. It's only a dream. It's me, Rand. Come on, wake up."

He knew the minute she became conscious of his presence. She immediately stiffened.

"You were having a nightmare, Lizbeth," he said, squeezing her hand. "Are you okay now?"

She hesitated only a second before surging up in bed and sliding her arms around his waist. "Oh, Rand," she whispered and burrowed her head against his shoulder.

She was terrified, he realized as she trembled against him. He continued to croon to her, nonessential words, while he held her soft body against his. To feel needed was heady and he cherished every moment of it as he gently rocked her back and forth.

Slowly, the trembling subsided. "I'm sorry. I guess the intruder triggered the nightmare. I thought… someone…had come after me to get me."

She didn't have to say Michael's name. Despite how pert she acted during the daytime, the man still obviously haunted her nights. "Well, no one's here, except me. Can you go back to sleep now?"

"Yes, of course," she said, gathering her shield about her. "I didn't mean to wake you."

He smiled. "No problem. I wasn't asleep."

"You having bad dreams, too?" she questioned.

"Actually, no, I was thinking about you."

There was a significant pause and he heard the sheet rustle as she shifted against the headboard. His arms felt empty without her. He yearned to take her in his arms and never let her go, but he ignored it. He had just promised himself he wasn't going to risk getting closer to her.

"Yes, you. Are you surprised you were on my mind?" he asked lightly. Knowing she wasn't over her fears and knowing he couldn't sleep while she was still frightened, he said, "Come on, I want some hot chocolate."

He didn't wait for her to respond but left her room and went down the stairs. He was glad to hear her follow. For once, she went to the cabinets and made the hot chocolate without giving him a lesson in where something was. When they were seated and had the hot chocolate in front of them he said, "I was thinking about our continued nipping at each other, first in the garden and then earlier tonight. I felt I should apologize. I know some of the things I said upset you."

"It's all right, Rand. I said things I shouldn't have said, either."

"We've only got a short time left together. You helped me a great deal, Elizabeth. I didn't think I was ready to learn, but looking back over the last weeks I guess that was why I was so frustrated when you first got here. I did want to learn but didn't think I could. I'm very appreciative of that. I don't want to ruin our last few days together because we have a difference of opinion."

"No, of course not. I've really enjoyed being here, too."

"Well, then," Rand said, strangely disappointed by her words. "Can we be friends then?"

"Of course," she agreed, sounding just as false as he had.

"Good."

"Yes."

There was a pause.

"Since we've got that cleared up," Elizabeth finally said into the awkward silence, "I'd like to ask you if you're willing to start using the cane."

Rand frowned.

"I know you don't like it but like you said, we've only got a short time left. I can always send someone else if you don't think I'm competent in that area."

"You know better than that."

"I know," she replied softly.

He sighed. "Stubborn wench," he muttered. "Fine. I suppose it won't hurt you to train me, in case I ever have to go out on my own voluntarily. But don't think I'm giving in. I can guarantee you I won't be going out on my own."

"Whatever," she said then changed the subject. "Have you heard from Max?"

"As a matter of fact, I did. I had four or five hang-up calls—probably that reporter, now that I think about it. You know, I just bet the reason he showed up is because I didn't answer the phone that last time. Anyway," he continued, getting his mind on his twin. "Max said that Colorado is a mess. They took the man into custody but didn't think he was a risk. So they let him out on bail and guess what?"

"Oh, no," Elizabeth murmured, leaning forward. "He didn't run, did he?"

"Oh, yeah. They aren't sure where. But the embezzlement is only a small part of what's up in Colorado. Max said it's been so long since we've been to the office there that the people have become lax. He has several things he said needed adjusting."

Elizabeth giggled. "I can just imagine what Max

wants to adjust, since he's not the people person in the business.''

''What makes you say that?'' Rand asked.

''Maybe because he loves numbers. And every time you mention Jennifer and work he gets this look of distaste on his face.''

Rand chuckled. ''I didn't realize it was that bad.''

''It could just be Jennifer and her crush,'' Elizabeth added, laughing.

Rand smiled. ''Yeah. Anyway, Max said he'll be there at least a week, maybe two. He promised to keep me updated, which means he'll probably call every day. He can be a mother hen even though he's younger.''

''By how long?'' she asked, laughing.

''Seven minutes.''

''Wow, seven minutes,'' she mocked.

''Actually, I tell everyone there's a day difference between us. You see, I was born just before midnight and he was born just after—one minute after, to be exact.''

''Poor Max. I'm beginning to think he deserves sainthood putting up with you.''

''If you only knew half of what he did to me you wouldn't say that,'' Rand complained good-naturedly.

''Yeah, sure. I wasn't born yesterday.''

''You were born...what? Twenty-eight years ago?''

''Thirty-two, I'll have you know. I'm not some spring chicken whose eyes you can pull the wool over.''

''Please, don't mention chickens. I think I've had my fill of them. And besides, chickens do *not* have wool.''

She laughed. ''Knock, knock.''

''Is this another chicken joke?'' he asked warily.

''Just answer,'' she admonished. ''Knock, knock.''

''Who's there?'' he said after a careful pause.

''Orange.''

"Orange?"

"No, you're suppose to say, 'Orange who?'"

"Okay, okay," he muttered. "Orange who?"

"Orange you glad I didn't do another chicken joke?"

He groaned, loudly. "I'm really beginning to hate chickens."

Her peals of laughter brought a smile to his face. "Why'd the bird cross the road?"

"Oh, no, you don't," he said, standing. "I refuse to hear—"

"Because it was stapled to the chicken!"

"Another chicken— That's it, you've done it now. I'm going to have to make you pay!"

She jumped from her chair, still laughing, and took off at a run through the house. He could hear her bumping into walls and furniture before she finally made it to the stairs.

He followed until he was at the bottom of the stairs. Her good-night floated to him, and he smiled.

Elizabeth was something else. Just when he was certain he had her pegged, she did something totally outrageous, like making him forget himself and chase her halfway across the house! He was lucky he hadn't broken his fool neck. Just like her. It was pitch-black in here, and she'd run through the house like she was blind.

"Well, I'll be..."

So, that had been a lesson, too, had it? He imagined she had been trying to boost his confidence.

Rand should be mad that she had used him like that, just to prove he wasn't as helpless as he thought.

But instead, he found he didn't mind at all.

He hoped the rest of her lessons turned out to be as much fun.

With a smile on his face he started up the steps. It

wouldn't do to let Sarah find him standing at the base of the steps in his pajama bottoms staring up the stairs like a lovesick fool. No, indeed.

Chapter Thirteen

❧

"This is totally ridiculous," Rand muttered as he bumped into a chair. "I was doing better before I started using the cane."

They had been working three hours, and Elizabeth was at her wits' end. "I think we've been working too long. It's very simple. Remember how I showed you if you go into an unfamiliar room to sweep your foot in front of you before you take a step. That's all you have to do with the cane. It's held out in front of you so you can feel the change in walking area or whatever."

Rand tossed the cane down, felt his way to the couch and sank wearily into its welcoming comfort. "I've had enough. You know, what I'd really like to do is go horseback riding. Unfortunately, you have to see to do that."

"You certainly are in one of your moods," she retorted. "Fine. You want to go horseback riding. Well, so do I. It's only been a few years. But if you were to ride double with me we could set a pace you just might enjoy."

For the first time that day the scowl disappeared off his face. "You're serious?"

"Sure. If you promise not to scowl once while we're out, I'll be happy to go."

"Good, let's go."

He stood and started toward the door.

"Aren't you forgetting something?" she asked sweetly and slapped the stick in his hand. "I told you I wanted you using this around the house for the entire week—regardless."

He growled, but took it and activated the small switch, then was out the door before she could say anything else.

Elizabeth ran quickly to the kitchen and grabbed some cheese and colas, a knife and some uncut salami. She wrapped it all in a fresh cloth sitting next to the dishwasher and was out the door, catching up with Rand before he had gone very far.

At the stables, the groom saddled a dappled mare that had a dainty look about her. "Go ahead," she said to Rand, helping him find his hold on the horse.

She saw the hesitation as he grabbed the saddle. Using her hands, she assisted in guiding him on. When he was seated, she grinned. "See, that wasn't so bad."

"I just love your sense of humor, Lizbeth," he grumbled, holding on to the horse as if it might bolt at any moment.

Elizabeth motioned to the groom, and he came over and helped her mount in front of Rand. "It would have been easier if you had gotten on first," Rand said when she settled herself in front of him.

"Whatever. Put your arms around me."

"Why, Ms. Jefferson," Rand drawled wickedly in her ear as he slid his arms around her tiny waist.

"Get any ideas, Mr. Stevens and I'd suggest you first remember who is holding the reins."

He chuckled and it vibrated through Elizabeth, warming her to the marrow of her bones. She hadn't thought about how close they would be while sharing the same saddle. She swallowed. This was not going to be as enjoyable as she had thought. Feeling perverse, she said, "By the way, did I tell you just how long it's been since I've actually ridden a horse?"

The smile left his voice. "How long?"

"Seventeen years." She clicked the horse into a trot, laughing at the way Rand suddenly leaned into her.

"You are kidding, aren't you?"

"I don't kid, at least about something like that. I remember it like it was yesterday. It was the summer I was fifteen. I decided to take riding lessons. Did I tell you about my broken collarbone?" she asked, all wide-eyed innocence even as the horse cleared the corral and headed across the field.

"A collarbone? I thought you broke it doing something else."

She laughed and urged the horse to a quicker gait. "Actually, I've been to the hospital fifteen different times. Some breaks were the same bones, some were multiple. In this case, the collarbone was a compound fracture. Hurt like the dickens. Had to have surgery. Long recovery time. But I had a good time that day—before the accident."

"How'd it happen?"

"I wasn't paying attention."

A low, heartfelt moan against her back was his answer.

"Don't worry, Rand, dahlin', I'll do my best to keep my eye on the trail."

"We don't have any horse trails on our property."

She made a show of looking around. "Oh, I see you're right. This is a pasture. Well, I'll keep an eye out for any cow paddies, how's that?"

"I'd rather you keep an eye out for any unusually large crawfish holes," he muttered, and she giggled.

"Relax. I'm much older now. I've been to the stable several times and I happen to know this little horse is one of the most tame animals you have. Why, I bet I could kick Buttercup in the sides until I bruised my heels and she wouldn't ever get up to a gallop."

"We don't have a horse called Buttercup."

"Oh, well, that wasn't originally the horse's name. However, I decided she was much too sweet for whatever it was, and so I gave her a new name. She likes it. I can tell."

"Yeah, uh-huh," he grumbled. "You are warped, dear lady," he mumbled, but that was the extent of his complaints. He rather liked her warped sense of humor. Slowly he relaxed and enjoyed the steady canter as they trotted across the fields. The horse's pace was relaxing. The wind gave him a sense of freedom. Peace stole over him as he held the petite woman in front of him. It gave him a sense of rightness, something he'd not felt in the last year and a half.

How could he let her leave in the next couple of weeks?

How could he not?

Before long they arrived at Elizabeth's destination. He heard the water before she had dismounted. "The stream?"

"Upstream, away from where we were last time we had a picnic. It's deep here. You can swim if you like. If we had bathing suits," she added, flustered. She re-

covered quickly. "Okay. I've got the horse's head, swing on down."

It was a lot easier getting up than getting down, Rand discovered. But with only minimal difficulty he slid to the ground. When he was sure his feet would hold his weight he turned. "Why did we stop here?"

"Lunchtime," she said with relish. "Salami, cheese and warm soda pop."

"Sounds delicious," he said, but meant just the opposite.

"Don't be a spoilsport." There was a pause. "Oh, dear."

"What?" he questioned.

"I forgot to pack plates," she replied, sounding not the least bit disturbed. "Oh, well, I have a knife.... I suppose I'll have to hand-feed you."

"Hand-feed me? You make me sound like a puppy or baby bird."

"You know that's not what I meant," she said lightly.

She took the saddle off the horse. He knew because he heard it hit the ground with a thud. And of course, he should mention all of her huffing and puffing just to tease her, but he didn't. "Why didn't you leave the saddle on?"

"Don't you know you're supposed to unsaddle a horse if it's left standing?"

"Only if we've been out here for hours and hours and are going to be spending the night."

"Oh," she said, nonplussed. "Oh, well, no problem. I'll resaddle it when we go. Come on. There's a tree over here."

She took his hand. He could feel the uneven ground and the tall grass brushing against his slacks. "Make sure there are no cow paddies,'' he murmured as she dragged him along.

She chuckled. ''You're so funny. Since there are no cattle in this field I doubt there are cow paddies.''

''Actually,'' he said, sitting down where she indicated, ''if you go on through the fields for a little bit I'm sure you'll see the cattle we own.''

''You own cattle?''

''They keep the grass down.''

A soda was thrust into his hands and then a piece of cheese. ''You hold those and I'll cut the meat.''

All was quiet for the moment, the only sound the wind and rustling of the leaves. Then she said, ''Open up,'' and promptly tried to stuff a piece of salami in his mouth.

''Raaful,'' he mumbled, pushing at her hand with his wrist.

She had the audacity to giggle. ''I'm sorry. I had nowhere to lay the knife when I poked the salami in your mouth.''

Swallowing, he said, ''You were holding a knife!''

''Wait a minute. Here, lay down, put your head in my lap and we can use your chest as a table.''

''Now you wait a minute,'' Rand protested.

''Well, I want to eat, too. And I am, after all, feeding you.''

Rand shook his head, exasperation and amusement warring with each other.

''Please,'' she cajoled.

''I want you to know I do this under protest.'' He held out the cheese and cola until she took it. He then turned until his head was in her lap. ''And don't try sawing a piece of that off while it's still on my chest.''

"I'd never do that," Elizabeth said, outrage in her voice.

"Well, with you, it never hurts to make sure."

She plunked the salami down, hard, across his abdomen. His breath whooshed out. "Watch it."

"Watch what?" she asked innocently. "Open up," she immediately said.

"You're so romantic. I'm not some trash processor, Elizabeth. Could you word that a little different?"

There was an ominously long pause, then she said, quietly, "Would you like some cheese, Rand?"

He was afraid to ask why she was being so nice instead of arguing with him.. "Yes," he finally said.

He parted his lips and waited. Then a feather light touch ran down his cheek, across his chin and to his other cheek. "How bad, Rand?"

"How bad what?" he asked, stunned by the sweet caress she was giving him and just a little wary. There was something about the caress that didn't feel exactly right, something...

"How bad do you want this cheese?"

"Cheese?"

A hand came up and he felt something go through his hair. He suddenly realized her game. He waited, forcing himself to forget about the tender caresses she was giving him. When she finally stopped and said, "Open up," he reached up, grabbed her arm and took the cheese from her.

"After you ran this through my hair? I don't think so."

She chuckled, a low, husky sound that reminded him how attracted he was to this woman. "I wouldn't really have made you eat the piece I did that with. It's over in the dirt. I just wanted you to take a bite and then I was going to tell you what I'd done and let you assume you were eating the piece I'd played around with.''

"You're sick, woman, real sick.''

"Here, eat this,'' she said and pushed a piece of cheese between his teeth.

"You know I'm going to have to bathe now that you've rubbed my lunch in my hair.''

"Really, Rand. You wanted romantic, not I.''

He didn't comment but enjoyed the silence as they both finished off the cheese and salami. And as they ate, Rand came to the conclusion that every event, whether large or small, would surely be a new adventure with this woman.

It was an hour later that someone slapped him on the leg. "Come on, lazybones, I know I work you hard, but I'm not a slave driver.''

Rand blinked, unable to believe he had fallen asleep. It must have been because he didn't get a good night's sleep.

"I wasn't sleeping, just resting,'' he grumbled, sitting up.

"Yeah, right. Well, it's midafternoon and we need to get back before someone sends out the National Guard for us. Can you gather up all of the trash and wrap it in the cloth lying by you? I'll saddle Buttercup.''

"Buttercup?'' he muttered, gathering everything around him. He still couldn't believe he had lowered his defenses enough to fall asleep with this woman sitting next to him.

He heard a thump and then a grunt. Pausing, he listened. Water splashed. "Will you just stand still, Buttercup?'' Elizabeth huffed as water splashed again. Evidently, the horse had backed into the creek.

He grinned, imagining her chasing the horse around as she tried to tighten the cinch. Quickly, he tied a knot in the cloth and then stood.

He edged his way toward the sound.

A loud exhalation and then, ''Well, we're ready.''

''I gathered as much,'' he said, his mood much improved.

''I've got the horse's head. You go ahead and climb up. Just come straight ahead. Oh, and be careful, the danged thing is standing right in the edge of the water.''

''Why don't you move her?''

''She's proving to be stubborn.''

''Ah,'' he said and chuckled.

He walked forward until he came to the side of the horse. ''Hold her steady,'' he warned and then, handing the bag of leftovers to Elizabeth, he grabbed the saddle and pulled. He was halfway up when he felt it slipping.

The horse shied and Rand knew he was going down. He kicked away from the horse.

Startled, the horse jerked and danced away. The water rose up to meet Rand.

With a loud splash, he landed on his rump in the water.

''Oh, no!'' Elizabeth shrieked and then there was a thump and thunder of hooves.

''Are you okay?'' Rand demanded, getting to his knees.

''I'm fine. The horse pulled away. I jumped and fell. I thought you might have been hurt.''

She splashed her way to him. When she was only a few feet away she chuckled. ''Well, it doesn't look like you need a bath now, Mr. Stevens. I'd say Buttercup made sure you had one.''

Her laugh was what did it. Hearing her standing over

him laughing because he'd fallen off a horse sparked some imp inside him. Before she knew what he was about, he reached out and snagged her leg. With a loud squawk she went down beside him.

When she came up sputtering he said blandly, "You should have warned me we were on Thunderbolt. I would have told you she likes to puff her sides out when you're cinching the saddle. It would have saved us both a bath."

Instead of getting angry, the way he thought she would, she chuckled ruefully. "Well, whatever. But I hate to tell you that Thunderbolt, aka Buttercup, left us behind so we've got a mile walk ahead of us."

He pushed himself up and waded out of the water.

"Then we'd better go, hadn't we?"

Elizabeth waded out of the water, too.

"How is it your ideal days outside the house always turn into adventures?" he asked as they began walking.

"Just lucky, I guess. Of course, from what you've told me, every time you and Max do something together you have quite an adventure yourself."

"That was ages ago," Rand said.

"Bet it wouldn't be if you two would take a break from work more often," she said.

They walked for about fifteen minutes in silence before Elizabeth spoke again. "I had planned on telling you earlier, but with all of the horseplay—"

He groaned.

"—I forgot."

When she hesitated Rand wondered if she had truly forgotten or was just nervous about telling him.

Then lightly, she said, "I had a call this morning, about another job."

Rand's heart plummeted at her words, but he didn't let it show. "Really?"

"A little girl. She is slowly losing her sight. They need someone to come in and work with her now, while she can still see."

"They can't fix the problem?"

"No. She was sick. It affected the nerves."

"How old is she?" Rand asked, the lump in his throat very real.

"Six."

He reached for Elizabeth's hand, wanting that contact, warring with his suddenly insecure feelings. He didn't want her to leave. He needed her. "She'll never see so many things," he murmured, thinking of the child. "She'll never see a football game at school, never see the senior prom. That's so young.... She won't ever know what a man she dates looks like, if she ever dates."

"It's hard," Elizabeth agreed. "But she'll find someone someday who loves her for herself, and it won't matter to them if she is blind or not."

"Yeah, Pollyanna," he muttered. She stiffened and he knew she heard what he'd called her, but he wasn't in a charitable mood at the moment. "I doubt there are many people who would want to be seen publicly dating someone like that."

"Why do you say that?" Elizabeth challenged.

"Let's face it. You can go out for a hamburger or maybe walking, but what about nice restaurants where the food isn't prepared just right, or a movie?"

"Blind people go to movies," Elizabeth retorted.

"But do their dates enjoy it?" he questioned stubbornly.

"I don't know," she replied mildly. "I've never been

on a date to a movie before, with a blind person, that is.''

"Fine,'' he said, and throwing all his earlier resolutions and cautions to the wind, he said, "you want to go with me?''

"What?'' She sounded startled.

"You heard me. I'm asking you out on a date tonight to go see the movie of your choice.''

Chapter Fourteen

Elizabeth looked at herself again in the mirror.

For Pete's sake. It was only an outing, not a real date. He had only used that word.

Still, she looked at the attempt to curl her hair and felt really stupid. Oh, it had turned out okay, she imagined. It was just that in the last ten years she had never, ever dressed up or curled her hair for *any* man.

She slid into the chair in front of her vanity. "How did you let Michael affect you so?" she asked herself.

Truth be told, she hadn't realized just how much her life had been wrapped up in the past. But Rand was changing all of that.

She touched the curls and thought about washing them out. But she looked so soft, feminine. And Rand probably wouldn't notice.

But he would smell her perfume, the one he had really seemed to like.

She was going to make a fool of herself, she just knew it.

She stood up.

She'd change. The jade sundress she was wearing was sleeveless and complemented her lightly tanned skin and red hair, and although he wouldn't know she was wearing it, she would.

She sat down.

She was being ridiculous.

So what if she had dressed up? She looked nice. And yes, she was dressing for a man. So what?

He's your patient.

But not for much longer, she argued with herself. And he wasn't really interested in dating.

But he asked you out.

Just to prove a point!

"Lizabeth?"

The voice from the other room decided everything for her. She had run out of time.

"Coming," she called, grabbing her purse.

Standing by her door was Rand. But it was a Rand she wasn't used to seeing.

Goodness, he looked gorgeous in those black pants and white shirt. She saw the shirt he was wearing was the one with the small silk stripes he'd worn the first day. And at his wrists were cuff links.

Cuff links!

See, he asked you out like a real date.

Unaware of Elizabeth's conflict, Rand slipped on his casual jacket and asked, "I didn't mismatch, did I?"

"You look—" She had to clear her throat. "You look fine."

"And what are you wearing?" he asked as he started down the hall.

"Oh," she said casually, "just a sundress. I thought it might be hot tonight."

He reached out and felt the soft material. "Just a sundress, huh? I'm going to have to examine your clothes to find out if your entire wardrobe is made out of this nice silky stuff.''

She blushed and promptly changed the subject. ''What did you want to see tonight?''

''How about the latest action adventure? That sounds about right up your alley.''

Relaxing at his banter, she replied, ''I dunno, maybe some really mushy movie that makes you cry in the end.''

''Save me from movies like that,'' he complained.

''Okay, okay, I give in. There is a really good action movie at the multiplex in town. Let's go there.''

They crossed the living room to the door and went out. Phil was there to drive them, and within a short time they were at the theater. ''We're about five minutes late,'' she said, looking at her watch.

''No lines, at least.''

He helped her out of the car. She could feel his tension. Despite his casual attitude he was beginning to have doubts. ''Don't worry,'' she said quietly as they walked to the window. ''You're going to enjoy yourself.''

''What movie?'' the teller asked.

Elizabeth told the young woman and pulled her purse off her shoulder. Rand's hand stopped her. ''My treat. I invited you, remember.''

He pulled out his wallet and she watched, with just a tinge of pride, as he felt his money and the different folds in each denomination and pulled out the correct amount to pay for the tickets.

''Can I treat us to popcorn?'' she asked as they entered.

''Do you think I'm a cheapskate?''

The process was repeated and then they were heading up the stairs to the theater where the show was already playing.

Inside, Elizabeth took a seat in the back row, which was almost empty. Rand eased down in the seat next to her.

"So, how does this work?" he asked.

"Listen," she replied. "I'll whisper and fill you in on any action."

She held out the popcorn and he took some. His eyes stared straight ahead and he sat tense as if afraid he might miss some small sound. Well, he would relax, Elizabeth imagined. Just give him a little time.

As the movie progressed Elizabeth leaned toward Rand and narrated as needed. She could smell his cologne, a musky, woodsy smell. It was very distracting and twice he had to ask her what had just happened. Elizabeth was lucky she could tell him because, leaning close to him the way she was, it was very hard to concentrate on the movie.

When the popcorn was gone, she set it and the drinks in the chair next to her. She leaned back, intending to stretch before beginning her narration again, but froze when she felt a brush against her shoulders.

Thinking it was a mouse, she jerked her head around, only to stare dumbfounded at Rand's arm.

"Elizabeth? Are you okay? You didn't answer my question."

"Your arm?" she blurted, and cringed when several people turned to look at her.

"What?" he whispered.

"Why's your arm behind me?" she whispered.

"Has it been that long since you've been out on a date, Lizabeth?"

Her eyes widened. "But this isn't a date, is it?"

Her voice had obviously risen again, because the people two rows in front of them glanced back.

"I distinctly remember asking you out. What did you think it was, if not a date?"

Elizabeth shifted. "You said yourself that you didn't want anything between us."

Rand turned to face her, lowering his head to her ear. "I did not say that, Lizabeth. I said I'd never take on the responsibility of someone again, as in marriage. I did not say I didn't want to date you, or other women."

Elizabeth knew her mouth was hanging open. She knew Rand had not said that to her. Maybe he had *decided* that, but he certainly hadn't *said* that. She would have remembered.

"If I made a mistake," he said, starting to pull back.

"No, it's okay. I, well, it's been a long time and I guess I'm a little rusty on picking up signals." Especially from a man who hadn't been over the death of his wife just three months ago, she thought, shaking her head in disbelief. The question she had to wonder about was, *Is he over her now?*

Then, despite the uproar on the screen a warm feeling spread through her. She was on a date, on an actual date. The first real date since Michael.

Oh, she'd gone out with a few other men, for dinner, but not when she was attracted to them. As a matter of fact, this was the first man she had ever been attracted to like this.

She felt his fingers brush her shoulder and was giddy. Heavens, it was like being seventeen years old again and wondering *Should I or should I not lean a little closer?*

She decided she should.

And she did.

Then shivered with delight when he pulled her just a bit closer, wrapping his arm around her shoulders.

She should remind herself that she was thirty-two. But this felt too wonderful to tell herself she shouldn't be doing it. After all, it was only a date. In a few weeks she wouldn't see him again.

The rest of the movie passed in a haze of pleasure, with her whispering narrative and answering questions. The occasional brush of his thumb against her neck or his lips against her ear caused her to lapse several times, and it took him asking her a question about the movie to remind her of her duty as narrator.

Still, she didn't think he was paying much attention to the movie, either. And when it was over, neither one moved from their seats. "I think it would be better if we waited until everyone else was out before we left," she said.

"As you wish," Rand replied. He finally removed his arm from around her only to slide it to her hand. He intertwined their fingers. "I'd like to take you out for coffee somewhere if you think you're up to it. I mean, I don't know how I'm going to look going in somewhere or what I might do."

"I don't mind," Elizabeth said softly, her other hand coming to rest on their intertwined fingers. "And you'll do fine."

"Yes, well..." He cleared his throat and stood. "You were right about the movie. I enjoyed it thoroughly." He gave her a wicked smile and she turned pink.

"So did I," she answered.

The last of the people were gone. She started to stand. "Just a minute," he said and leaned forward.

His lips touched hers lightly, just a brush, once, twice,

a third time and then he pulled back. "I've wanted to do that all evening."

"I've wanted you to do that all evening," she replied.

He smiled, then it faded. "I don't know what's happening here, Elizabeth. I will tell you that I never expected to get out of my house again. And I can guarantee you that I'll never marry again. I couldn't ask that of anyone. A woman deserves more, a chance to experience life, a life she couldn't experience with a blind man. And she deserves to feel protected, something I'd be totally incapable of doing."

She started to speak but his fingers over her lips stopped her. "Anyway, like I said, this is very unexpected. I've been fighting the feelings for you since the first day you walked into my room. I'm tired of fighting. I'd like your permission to ask you out again."

Elizabeth blinked.

That had been a very blunt speech, she thought. He wanted to date her. But that was all. She knew he still had a lot of things to work through, the main one of which was forgiveness and acceptance of himself.

Did she want to get tangled up in all of this?

She had problems that were just coming to light, problems in the way she looked at herself.

But Rand had changed her whole outlook. Without his help she might never have stepped out of that ice-encased shell where she'd been hiding and experienced the joy of trusting a man again.

And she did trust Rand.

There was no doubt about that.

Yet, when she thought about it, she wondered if there was really a choice to make. Their lives were already intertwined in some indelible way that she couldn't explain.

"I would very much like it if you'd ask me out again, Rand Stevens."

His shoulders relaxed as if some huge weight was suddenly gone. A smile spread across his face. "Come on, then, let's go get that coffee."

As they had been at the last movie of the night, there were few people hovering and even fewer cars. She pushed open the door as they walked out. "Phil is straight ahead," she said, spotting the oversized car in the parking lot.

So intent was she on reaching the limo she almost missed seeing the sedan come around the corner of the theater. She turned her head, slowing her walk to see what had caught her attention in her peripheral vision.

Everything happened at once.

Phil, who was standing by the car, called out, "Good movie, Mr. Stevens?"

Rand, not realizing or understanding that Elizabeth had slowed, or why, continued toward the car.

The person in the oncoming vehicle floored the gas, intent on running them down.

Without thinking, Elizabeth made a flying leap at the unsuspecting Rand.

"Rand!" she screamed.

Her body connected against his with a loud thud. They went down together and rolled across the pavement.

Pain exploded through Elizabeth's body.

The sedan missed. But she felt the whoosh as it skimmed by them.

"Mr. Stevens!" Phil yelled in his British accent. "Are you and Ms. Jefferson okay?"

"Elizabeth?" Rand asked, moving his hands over her. "Elizabeth, honey, are you okay?"

"Yeah," she finally said, pushing herself up. She

noted a small crowd had gathered about them. "I just feel like I've gone ten rounds with a Mack truck, and lost, though."

"Oh, Ms. Jefferson, that shoulder looks pretty bad," Phil said.

She scowled at him when Rand's frown turned foreboding. "Just road rash. I scraped a few layers of skin off."

"Likely it's going to be bruised, and bad," Phil continued, ignoring Elizabeth's warning frown to be quiet and turning to Rand to help him up. "I saw her hit, and all of her weight came down on that shoulder. That person tried to run you down."

Reaction was setting in, and suddenly Elizabeth's anger faded, only to be replaced by weakness. She felt like a leaf in the wind, shaking so thoroughly that she was certain a wind could blow her away.

"She's looking peaked, Mr. Stevens," Phil warned.

Rand's arm was suddenly around her. "Get us to the car," he said.

"I'm okay, really," she protested weakly, but she limped, every muscle in her body beginning to protest movement as the adrenaline wore off.

"I'm the manager," a young man said, stepping forward. "Is there anything we can do?"

"Yes," Rand replied. "Call the police. Phil will give you our address. I'm taking Ms. Jefferson to a hospital—"

"No, Rand. I'm fine."

"I insist."

"I refuse."

"Fine. I'm taking you home. If the police have any questions they can contact us there."

He got into the car while Phil gave the manager of the theater all the information.

Rand sat in one corner of the car. "Put your head in my lap. Phil said you didn't look good and I don't want to feel you suddenly slumping from a faint."

"I don't faint," Elizabeth said indignantly, but she had to admit she felt like she might just about now. That's the reason she didn't argue and wilted against the soft leather seats.

"How bad is your shoulder?" Rand questioned, concern in his voice.

"I'm not going to bleed on the car—much," she quipped.

"I don't care about the car," he said harshly. "It's you I'm worried about."

"I know," she replied quietly, and then began to shake. "I thought you were going to die tonight. I just happened to catch a movement from the corner of my eye. I hesitated, something warning me, and then that madman floored it. The tires came within inches of us."

And that was when Elizabeth Jefferson had realized something very, very important.

She loved Rand Stevens. With all of her heart she had fallen inexorably in love with the hardheaded fool.

And he wanted nothing to do with love or marriage.

What a tangled mess we have, she thought dispiritedly.

Oh, Father, she said silently. *What is going to happen now?*

Long, strong fingers stroked the waves of hair over and over again as Elizabeth lay there. At some point, she noted the tall, lean silhouette as Phil climbed into the car and drove off, but Elizabeth wasn't paying much attention to that. Instead, she was concentrating on a tension that was continuing to build in Rand.

"What is it, Rand?" she finally asked.

"Nothing."

"Yes, there is something," she said, attempting to push herself up, but he wouldn't let her.

"Lie still."

"Only if you tell me what's eating at you."

"You could have been killed," he finally said savagely.

"I think we've covered that already," she replied dryly.

"And there was nothing I could do to protect you."

Oh, boy. You should have seen this coming, Elizabeth, she admonished herself.

"Rand," she began, but he interrupted.

"I didn't even know the car was there. We both could have been killed."

"But we weren't. And Rand," she said, forcing herself into a sitting position despite his protests, "I don't think this was an accident. The person waited until you were out in the middle of the road before he sped up."

Rand frowned. "Why would anybody want me dead?" he asked finally.

Elizabeth shifted. "I don't know, but someone obviously does. And if I were you, I'd be thinking awfully hard of who might have a motive to hurt you."

Chapter Fifteen

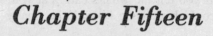

"Richard Warren," Rand said as they sat in the kitchen letting Sarah tend to Elizabeth's shoulder.

"What?" Elizabeth asked, wincing when Sarah began applying the salve.

"The person who might want me dead."

Sarah finished the salve and then wrapped Elizabeth's arm with a gauzy pad. "I'm going to feel like a mummy, Sarah, if you put much more of that on me."

"It's just for tonight. It'll keep those wounds from seeping all over the bed. My lands, girl, between your shoulder, your elbow and that right knee of yours, your sheets would be a mess in the morning."

"She's in a mess right now," Rand muttered, distracted from what he had been about to say. "And I imagine by tomorrow she's not going to be able to move."

"Humph," Sarah said, expressing her opinion. "She can't hardly move now, Mr. Stevens. I think she should have gone to the hospital. Maybe my husband and I should cancel our vacation. You two certainly need us more—''

"Really, you two," Elizabeth complained to Rand and the housekeeper. "All they would have done was give me some pain medicine. I can take a couple of over-the-counter pills for that and be fine."

"We'll see how fine in the morning," Rand growled.

"All done," Sarah said. "You want me to help you upstairs?"

"That won't be necessary," Rand interrupted. "Thank you for your assistance. I wasn't sure if you'd be here tonight or out on the town with that husband of yours."

Sarah laughed like a schoolgirl. "You and your brother are something else, Mr. Stevens. Go on. Off to bed. I'll see you in the morning."

She left, going to the suite off the kitchen wing she and her husband had lived in for over fifteen years.

Rand helped Elizabeth stand. Unwillingly a groan escaped her lips. "I'm going to hurt tomorrow, there's no doubt about that," she said as she started toward the stairs. "Now tell me, who is Richard Warren?"

"The man Max said is embezzling from the business."

"Oh, dear," Elizabeth said, pausing at the bottom of the stairs. "You don't think he's made it all the way to Louisiana, do you?"

Rand's face was grim. "He's the only one I can think of who might have a remote possibility of wanting to run me down. After we get you in bed I'm going to call Max and get an update on what they know about Richard's whereabouts and just how much he's purported to have embezzled."

"But you said he was a friend!" Elizabeth said, dismayed.

"He was. But people will do all sorts of things for money. And as I said, he's the only one I can think of who has a grudge against me. Now, come on, it's up the stairs for you."

Elizabeth toddled up the stairs like an eighty-year-old woman, each step hurting her bruised hip. Rand was patient, taking his time, assisting her until they reached the top.

When they entered her room, he paused at her door. "Can you manage?"

She smiled. "Actually, maybe Sarah should have come up with me. This dress zips and there is no way I'm going to be able to contort my body to reach this zipper feeling like I am."

"Oh." Rand stood undecided a moment, then shrugged. "Turn around."

"Rand," Elizabeth said, suddenly embarrassed.

"It's not like I'm going to see anything," he mocked.

A small chuckle escaped. She turned. "Yeah, right. You people who are blind sometimes see much more than someone with two good eyes."

Rand slipped the zipper down, but when Elizabeth started to move away, he stopped her.

"If you need anything, Lizbeth, anything at all, I'm right across the hall."

Tears sprang to her eyes. The attendant had suddenly become the one tended to, and by the patient, no less. "Thank you, Rand. And good night."

"Good night."

She watched him walk away, thinking how much she wished he'd kissed her good-night. Of course, that would have been ridiculous considering how sore she was, and because she had allowed him to unzip her dress and now stood there with her clothes barely hanging on her.

With a sigh, she went into her room and closed the door.

Rand's mind was far away from romance and kisses. His mind was on the bruised body sleeping across the hall from him. He was furious over his inability to protect the woman when she had needed it. And he wanted to make whoever was responsible pay. He couldn't physically beat the person to a pulp, since he didn't even know who the person was—and even if he knew, he couldn't see him. He would retaliate the only way he could. He would find out who was responsible and see him in prison.

He picked up the phone and dialed Max in Colorado.

"Hello?"

"Max, this is Rand."

"I had a feeling you would be calling."

Rand sighed. Slipping off his cuff links, he placed them on the bedside table. He was not surprised that Max had picked up on his anxiety.

"So, what happened? It's past midnight there so I know you wouldn't be calling just to reassure me you're okay."

"Someone tried to run me down tonight."

"As in hit and run?" He heard the surprise in Max's voice. If that surprised him, the rest of the story really would.

"I was at a movie."

"Oh, boy, let me sit down," Max said. "Now, you want to run that by me again?"

"I took Elizabeth out to a movie. It's that simple."

"*You* took *Elizabeth* out. Wait, we can discuss that

later," he said, definitely sounding like he'd been thrown a curve ball. "Okay, you're at the movie theater and then what?"

"Elizabeth and I came walking out. I heard Phil call out asking about the movie and started toward his voice. I guess for a minute there I forgot I was blind," he said sarcastically. "The next thing I know, Elizabeth screams my name and knocks me over with a flying tackle."

"Man, bro, are you okay?"

"I am. Elizabeth is pretty banged up. She had on this nice little sundress that left her arms bare. Unfortunately, she landed on her right shoulder and elbow and knee and who knows what else that she has failed to mention to me. I only know of those because of what Phil and Sarah have told me. She's as sore as if she's been kicked by a horse—or worse."

"I can see this is pretty serious. I'll leave the rest for when I get home. What do the police say?"

"I don't know. Phil took care of that. I'll either have to go down tomorrow and talk to them or they'll come out here. I've been trying to think of who might have a motive to hurt me."

"It's been awhile since you've been involved in the business. Except for a few retailers that were in trouble that we bought out, I can't think of anyone who might be angry with you."

"I've thought of a couple of people."

"Who?"

"Well, the kid's family that ran Carolyn and me off the road."

"But why? He was drunk and at fault."

Rand shrugged. "Yeah, I pretty much discarded that idea. But what about Richard?"

"Richard Warren?"

"Yeah. He *is* missing. Is it possible he's angry enough—"

"We've known him our whole life, Rand. I sure don't like to think he's capable of something like that."

"Neither do I." Rand sat down and removed his shoes. "But I want to find whoever it is. They almost killed Elizabeth tonight. I want them to pay. I don't think I could stand it if something happened to her. The trouble is, even though I can't imagine Warren doing something like this, he is the only one I can think of. He's scared and possibly angry at us for discovering his embezzlement scheme."

Rand finished removing his shoes and started on his shirt before he realized there was a silence on the other end of the phone.

"So," Max finally said. "It's like that, is it?"

"What?" Rand asked.

"You and Elizabeth."

"I don't catch the drift, brother."

"You're in love with her."

"No way!"

"Yes, brother. It certainly sounds like it to me." His Cajun accent was obvious, a warning that Max was definitely enjoying his guess.

Rand shifted the phone to his other hand and picked up his clothes. He took them to the laundry baskets and dumped them in. "It's not like that at all. Okay, okay," he said when Max started to argue. "We are attracted to each other, but it won't go beyond that."

"Why not?" Max asked bluntly.

"Why not?" Rand echoed. "I'm blind, that's why not."

"And?"

"Well, take tonight as an example, if the fact that I'm

blind isn't enough. I won't risk putting her in danger. It's happened once. Never again."

Max sighed, exasperated. "You know, Rand, you're gonna have to stop playing God."

"Now just a min—"

"Hear me out, brother. I mean it. You've always been a control nut. It's time you realized you can't always be in control."

"Don't you think I realize that?" Rand whispered, a tortured sound to his voice.

"You may realize you haven't been in control, like when Carolyn died, but you haven't realized that you can't control everything. Accidents happen. Sometimes we don't understand why. But they do happen. It's times like those we just have to trust God, let Him help us through the hard times, then pick ourselves up and go on. You can't continue to hide behind your guilt at being out of control. Carolyn wouldn't want that. I certainly don't want that. And God doesn't want that."

"I don't know if I can step out and just trust everything to fate like you want, Max."

"I'm not asking you to do what I want. I'm asking you to talk to God and let Him change you. I'm telling you, bro, you can't do any better than Elizabeth. She's a good woman, really loves God and needs someone like you in her life."

"I don't know," Rand said again.

"Well, anyway, I'll check with the police here and have them contact the Baton Rouge police department. We'll find out what we can. And in the meantime..."

"Yes?" Rand asked when Max paused.

"Stay out of sight."

"I didn't think I'd ever hear you telling me to hide," Rand said.

Max chuckled wryly. "Well, there's always a first time for everything. Take care."

"Yeah, you, too."

He placed the phone in the cradle and finished putting everything away in his room. He had learned quickly that to leave anything out proved hazardous to his health.

When he was done he went in and showered, hoping to relieve the soreness he was experiencing from hitting the pavement so hard. Yeah, he was sore, but nothing like Elizabeth. He was afraid he might have squished her in the fall. He had tried to twist and cushion her but obviously he hadn't been entirely successful.

Out of the shower, he dressed in his pajama bottoms and crawled in bed. Stacking his hands behind his head he thought about what Max had said.

He didn't like the picture Max had painted. He did enjoy Elizabeth's company, was beginning to think he could really care for her if things were different. But Max wanted him to look past his blindness, hope for something that, in Rand's opinion, couldn't be. Elizabeth had asked him to do that by going to a movie tonight.

And for a short time it had been wonderful. The date had reminded him of when he'd first started dating Carolyn. Except where Carolyn had been very sure of herself, Elizabeth had been unsure, shy, even a little wary at first.

He had thoroughly enjoyed experiencing the joy of playing the dating game. Elizabeth was a wonderful person, had done marvels with him. As an individual, she had gone through so much and come out still fighting.

She was the type of person who was loyal, and once her heart was given, she would love with everything inside her. You could hear it in her voice. He'd wanted to talk to her the other day and had gone to her door to knock. He'd paused when he heard her talking, though, only to realize she was praying.

Praying.

And not like so many people. To her, God was real. She was having an argument over whether or not she should force him to use a cane, which included a suggestion of ramming it down his throat.

Rand smiled at the memory. The woman was something else. Her simple belief, so strong, was almost enough to persuade him that his handicap didn't matter, that he could traverse it and win.

He thought of her in bed across the hall, and what she'd gone through tonight, and remembered her pain as she had hobbled up the stairs.

In that one moment he was reminded of how impossible it would be for him to even hope for anything more than a simple friendship with an occasional date.

Which was just as well.

He needed reminding. He couldn't lose sight of that, no matter how he might feel for her. Elizabeth was a chance taker, and if she got serious about him, she would not think twice about marrying him even though he was blind. She wouldn't think anything could happen to her, or him. Look at all the accidents she'd had as a child, and she had just gone on to something else, only to be hurt again.

Rand had learned the hard way that lessons should be remembered. He would not risk getting serious about Elizabeth.

No, his brother was wrong when he said Rand was in love with Elizabeth. Rand knew better than to risk his heart.

And if he kept telling himself that, maybe he could convince himself before he had to face her in the morning.

Chapter Sixteen

"Lizabeth?"

Elizabeth heard Rand's tentative call and started to sit up. She fell back, groaning instead.

"Can I come in? I've brought you breakfast in bed."

Elizabeth edged her sore body up in the bed until her back was against the headboard. "Come on in, Rand. You shouldn't have done that."

She watched him carry in a filled tray, delicious aromas wafting from it.

"How are you feeling?"

"Sore," she said, groaning as she stretched to receive the tray from Rand's hands.

He seated himself in a chair next to her bed and clasped his hands between his knees.

"Join me?" she asked.

"I've already eaten. I was up early. Max called."

Elizabeth nibbled on a piece of toast, not really very hungry. "Oh?" she questioned. "What was it he wanted?"

"He wanted to let me know that the police here in

Baton Rouge have been contacted with a description of Richard Warren. If he's the man who tried to run us down they'll probably be able to track him pretty quickly.''

''Well, that's good news, if not perfect,'' she said, and took a sip of her juice.

Pushing her tray away, she asked Rand, ''Do you feel like going out today or do you want to stay closer to the house?''

''I think the house,'' he murmured, a frown on his brow.

''Then how about a swim and then you can work some in your office? That way, if you have any questions about anything I'll be here to answer them.''

''That sounds good. Are you going to finish eating?''

''Don't sound so concerned,'' Elizabeth said, swinging her legs off the bed, ''I'll be famished by lunch. Now go. It's indecent that I let you sit in here with me while I'm still in bed.''

Rand's frown disappeared for the first time since he'd entered her room. ''It's not like I can see anything.''

''Go *on*,'' she said, chuckling. When he was gone, her chuckles disappeared and were replaced with several groans as she got up and slipped into her bathing suit.

She noted her body was black and blue. Still, at least she didn't have any broken bones. Going into the main room, she sat by the window while she did her morning devotions then, after returning her Bible to her room, she went downstairs. Rand was already in the pool, swimming laps.

She eased her body into the warm water. Though she thought she'd made no sound, Rand swam toward the shallow end and stood. ''How many laps are you up to today?'' he asked.

"Five?" she said, crossing her fingers. She'd be lucky to get three in.

"Done that," he murmured, coming to stand in front of her. "How about I do five more with you...just in case you get in trouble," he teased.

"Okay, wise guy, you're really pushing it. I'm fine. I'll have no problem with five laps."

They both took off at a steady pace. Rand easily out-distanced her but purposely held back when she fell behind. It was a companionable time, a time to work out, enjoy the peace and clear their minds of any problems. And last night was one of her biggest problems so far. It had been downright scary thinking she might lose Rand. It was something she never wanted to witness again.

"You're tired."

Hearing Rand's voice, she stood up in the shallow end. "Four laps isn't bad," she defended herself, though she could usually do ten easily.

Rand came over to her. Elizabeth held her breath. He raised his hands and found her shoulders, gently tracing the injury on her right one. "It's a mess," he said, his voice a gentle caress, full of tender concern.

"It'll heal in a few days. Really," she reassured him when his frown returned. "I'm fine."

"Well, we certainly won't be going out on a date tonight," he muttered.

"Why, Rand?" Elizabeth questioned, hoping this in-cident hadn't set back his confidence in himself. "Is it because of my injuries or do you fear being unable to protect me?"

Rand scowled. "You know it's both."

"I figured as much. Rand, I wish you could understand that you can't control situations. Sometimes you just have to leave it all in God's hands."

"Elizabeth," he warned.

"Okay, okay." She sighed. "How about pizza tonight? We can play a board game, or maybe rent a movie."

"You don't give up, do you?" he asked, though his voice was tinged with amusement.

"I'm very stubborn. And I want to be with you."

He raised an eyebrow. "What about that patient versus dating theory you had?"

"It's been blown away by my desire to spend time with you."

Rand grinned very arrogantly.

"I knew I shouldn't have told you. You'll be impossible to live with the rest of the month."

His smile slowly faded. "That's when you're leaving?"

Her own smile disappeared. "Yes."

He nodded. Turning toward the stairs he said, "Actually, that's for the best. I don't want you in the way while this maniac is chasing after me. You might think about leaving before then."

She was stunned. "Rand!"

"Look, I'm going into the office. If you have any errands you need to run, why don't you go out now and get them out of the way?"

He didn't wait to hear her reply.

Elizabeth watched him go, depressed. He was so touchy. The least little hint that he wasn't in control and he stormed off.

She sighed as she got out of the pool and dried off. You would think, after all he had been through, that he would have accepted that no one can be in complete control. Of course, she admitted reluctantly, he *had* known that, and hidden behind that when she'd first arrived. It was only now that he had control in some parts of his life that he stubbornly insisted on wanting complete control again.

Maybe he didn't realize that was what his problem was. But it was. She didn't know how to make him understand that blind or not, people just couldn't control everything. Or maybe that was it. Maybe deep down he knew that, and that was why he kept pushing her away. Not because of his blindness but because he knew there were no guarantees and he wasn't going to risk the pain again.

She sighed. He had talked about *her* sending out mixed signals not too long ago. He was worse than she ever dreamed of being. He wanted her, he was attracted to her, he might even love her if his concern and tender looks were any indication, but he wouldn't allow her into his life.

Going into the house, she decided to dress and go by her house. She hadn't been there in two days and needed to pick up the mail and check on things. Maybe that would give Rand and her both the time they needed from each other.

Rand sat in his office in front of his computer. He'd been there for over an hour and hadn't gotten a single thing done.

Nope.

His mind kept replaying the scene in the pool this morning.

Elizabeth obviously wanted more from their relationship than he could give her. So did he. He would love to cherish her forever. But just the thought terrified him.

How could he hold on to her and love her when he couldn't take care of himself? If he thought of what the next ten years of his life would look like, he imagined Elizabeth and him together. She would be outgoing, thriving on adventure, wanting to go skydiving and snorkeling and just about anything else he could imagine. He would be on the sidelines. She would want him to be with her, but there were certain limitations to having no sight. And Elizabeth, loving him as she would, would give up those chances to take care of him.

The thoughts were humiliating.

However, if he tried to picture his life ten years from now without her, all he could envision was a bleak, empty desert with his days spent in the house with no one around him. Oh, his brother, Max, would be there for awhile yet. But what about when Max married?

Both outlooks were unacceptable.

So what was he going to do? He had to change one. But which one? Was it possible for him and Elizabeth to develop some sort of relationship where they could coexist together and not have resentment eventually take its toll?

Could he go back to work and form some friendships outside of this house with people who would understand his limitations and not pity him?

He rested his head in his hands.

Both scenarios had no answers. Both required he take a chance. The latter guaranteed he wouldn't have to risk someone getting hurt because of him, but he could not imagine being alone the rest of his life, dying of loneliness.

The former is what his heart wanted, but could he open himself up again to losing someone? The guilt of Carolyn's death washed over him and he clenched his hands. She had been so alive, so ready for all life had to offer. Why had he insisted his way was the only way? Why had he been so confident that he could handle anything that was tossed at him?

Elizabeth's faceless form superimposed itself over Carolyn's lifeless body as it had hung in the car, in her seat belt, forever denied the experience of children and a future.

He sucked in a harsh breath. He couldn't face that possibility.

I'm here for you.

He heard the whisper, but denied it. "I can't. It's my fault," he whispered to the voice.

Come to Me with your burdens, I will give you peace.

"Peace?" He laughed, though it sounded harsh. "Why do I need peace? What good would it do?" he asked God, his voice thick with anguish. "Peace won't give my wife a second chance. Peace won't give Elizabeth a chance with true happiness. She needs someone who can do what she enjoys, who can watch out for her when she's out getting into accidents. She doesn't need someone who is just as likely to fall off a horse because he doesn't *see* the cinch is loose or gets turned around in a pool simply because he wasn't paying attention to what he was doing. Peace isn't for me."

He slammed his fists against the desk and stood. The small, gentle voice had been getting more insistent lately. It was tearing Rand apart to hear the compassionate suggestions that he fall down on his face and cry his heart out to God. He didn't deserve to be let off so easily for the atrocities he'd caused.

And even if he did find some sort of peace, then what? What next? There was that big unknown again. His whole life had ended in the accident. What would he do if he decided to continue on?

His life was like a shattered crystal goblet, laying about his feet in millions of fragile pieces. It would be impossible to put them back together. Carolyn was dead. He was blind.

How was he to find another goblet and start anew?

To his way of thinking, it was impossible. A wide open fissure stretched out before him. He didn't think he could step out in it in faith and just believe everything would go onward.

Furious with the way his mind was going in circles, he went downstairs to get himself a glass of milk and some of the cookies Sarah had baked. She and her husband were leaving this evening for their two-week vacation. She'd been telling Elizabeth only yesterday that they were going to the Grand Canyon. They'd always wanted to see it. And as was Sarah's custom, she had made enough cookies and brownies to turn both he and Max into Pillsbury dough boys by the time she got back.

The freezer would be full of casseroles with the heating instructions on them. Sarah was awful about spoiling them. She'd offered to cancel her vacation, or hire someone to come in.

Rand had declined. He wanted this last week with Elizabeth. Of course, now that he had told her to leave early, he might find himself alone.

A daunting prospect, since they'd only spent three days in the kitchen learning the basics about warming up things in the microwave.

Still, so be it. If Elizabeth decided to leave him, it might just be for the best.

In the kitchen he found a glass and the milk and was

pouring it when the back door slammed. He felt his watch. It wasn't Sarah—it was too early.

"Elizabeth?" he called.

He heard footfalls, and immediately recognized Elizabeth's tread.

"I'm back earlier than I intended. Ah, so you're having cookies, are you? I passed Sarah and told her not to worry about dinner tonight, to go ahead and get an early start. I also picked up your mail."

He heard the slap of an envelope on the table.

"Wanna share?" she asked, coming over and scooping up a cookie. "Mmm."

His tension melted away as he listened to her chatter. "Help yourself." He sat at the table. "The mail was brought up earlier. Was this UPS?"

"I don't know. It was just sticking out of the mailbox. It's a manila envelope."

Rand felt the oversize envelope and frowned. "Who's it from? Maybe Max sent me something."

"No. The postmark is Baton Rouge."

Rand shrugged and slipped his finger beneath the flap. He slit it opened and reached inside. Polished cool papers slid into his hand. "These aren't made of regular paper," he said.

Elizabeth gasped, latching onto his arm.

"What?" he demanded, her fear communicating itself to him. "What is it?"

"I don't believe this. Rand, they're pictures of us." She took the photographs from his hands. "This one is of us eating at Mama Ria's." She passed him a photo. "And this one is of us at your work being mobbed by reporters."

Rand scowled. "Probably that idiot that was arrested the other day trespassing."

"Oh, my heavens. I hope you're right, because this is one of us swimming and one of us... Oh, dear, remember when you kissed me in the pool?"

Rand grabbed the picture, feeling violated. "I'll sue that guy," he muttered furiously.

"Oh, no."

"What else?" he asked, resigned.

"Rand, it couldn't have been that reporter."

"Why not?" A cold chill worked its way down his spine at the certainty in her voice.

"Because here is a picture taken only two days ago. Rand, the police had the photographer in custody by then."

Rand stilled. "Give me those pictures."

"Why?"

"Because I think this means another call to my lawyer."

"Are you sure about this?"

"I'm sure, Elizabeth."

"Oh, my lands," she whispered.

"Yeah, oh, my lands," he muttered.

"Do you really have to involve your lawyer?"

"After almost getting run down the other night and now these pictures... I just don't think we need to be taking any more chances. I want my lawyer to take a look and try to find out what's going on. Whoever this is, they're serious. They're following us, keeping a close watch on us. And I have no idea who it could be."

Rand stood and headed toward his office. "Stay right there, Elizabeth. I have a few more questions I need to ask you."

Numbly, Elizabeth nodded. She wasn't going anywhere, not until she had some answers about what was going on and why everything seemed to be spinning suddenly out of control.

Chapter Seventeen

"Well, the lawyer thinks it's probably a nut case."

"So it's not Warren?"

"No. Definitely not. The lawyer just informed me he was recaptured. Evidently, the phone people have been working in the area and Max had trouble getting through to us. And since my cellular is still in my room…"

"I'll tell you something, Rand. When things go crazy around you, they really go crazy. You never do anything halfway. So, what are we going to do?"

"My lawyer suggested we wait it out. He asked if I was dating the person in the picture. He hypothesized maybe the nut was a woman who had become enamored with my situation and didn't like it that I was no longer a helpless victim she could moon over."

"He's not serious, is he? Do you believe this?"

"Yes, he was serious. No, I don't believe it but I don't have any other explanation. However, the lawyer's idea *is* a pretty common occurrence. You take someone who's in the news a lot and set it up where they look like a tragedy that everyone can cry over. You'd be surprised how much mail that person will get.''

"You?"

"Yep. Max read the serious letters and forwarded any that sounded suspicious to our lawyer. Since we haven't had any problems before, nothing has been done. The lawyer is going to check out all the mail right now."

"Then he also thinks that last night—"

"Yeah. If I ticked someone off they might have been trying to warn me."

"They were trying to kill you!"

"The lawyer doesn't think so. After all, running someone down in a movie parking lot is not the ideal way to murder someone."

"We're not talking about a sane person."

"I honestly don't think the lawyer is on the right track." Rand sat. Running a hand through his hair, he frowned. "Something doesn't fit. If a woman was angry at me dating you, why would she run me down instead of you?"

Elizabeth nodded. "You're right. It'd make more sense to go after me. So, if it's not an accountant or a crazy letter writer, then who is it?"

"I just don't know," Rand muttered. "I have no enemies that I know of. But my lawyer is looking into any possibility. He's promised to get back to me as soon as possible. In the meantime, I'd ask you to be a little more careful about leaving the house."

Elizabeth fixed their dinner, which they ate in the dining room. Afterward Rand sat back, more contented than he had been in a long time.

"I want to find the book on tape that Max bought me several months ago. Would you help me find it?" Rand asked Elizabeth.

"Sure," Elizabeth replied. "Do you have any idea where it might be?"

"The library, if I know Max." Rand picked up his cane, which Elizabeth insisted he use, and they went to the library together. She walked into the room only to stop short. "Well, I see where you keep all of the family pictures," she murmured, smiling.

"Oh, yeah," Rand said, sounding ill at ease.

Elizabeth heard his tone but didn't immediately comment. Instead, she began to search until she found the tape. When Rand started to leave, Elizabeth said softly, "She was very beautiful."

Rand paused, giving her an inscrutable look. "Yes, she was."

"What was she like?"

"Special."

"I know that," Elizabeth said, then chuckled. "I just wanted to know what she was like."

"Why?"

"Just curious. I figure she had to be pretty special to grab you."

He laughed, but there was a haunted look in his eyes.

"Look, I'm sorry," Elizabeth said. "I didn't mean to bring up any bad memories."

"Oh, they're not bad." He sighed, his shoulders slumping. Wistfully he said, "Bittersweet would be a better word. Sweet because they're mostly fond, bitter because she'll never be back."

He came back into the library and sat on the couch. "I guess I'm starting to accept that," he said. "No, I *have* accepted that," he amended, slightly astonished. "It doesn't hurt as much any more."

Elizabeth silently slid onto the couch near him. He stared off into space, and she was certain he was remembering the good and bad times he'd had with his wife.

"We had a friendship that floated into love. On my part at least. Carolyn always had a bold assurance that she had my attention." He laughed and shook his head. "I imagine I was pretty pathetic the way I followed her around."

"It sounds cute."

"Max didn't think so. He said I looked ridiculous. And he was right. But I didn't care."

He stretched out his legs, relaxing against the soft sofa. "We were both go-getters. Actually," he said, a small frown dimming his smile, "we both led very busy lives and didn't have much time together. We were too busy planning out how to live our lives to the fullest."

He paused. "I've really enjoyed these past two months. Not all the therapy," he explained. "But getting out and learning things over again." He shook his head. "I don't know that Carolyn and I ever took time to listen to a bird."

A sad smile crossed his face. "It didn't mean I didn't love her. We both had the same goals. We wanted to make a go of the business, increase the profits, have something really productive for the kids we would one day have. Carolyn had planned to take time off when she had kids. But you know, looking back, I can't imagine her ever staying at home. She was too involved in the business to take a back seat."

"Would you have minded if she had continued to work?"

Rand frowned. "I don't know. Maybe we both could have worked it out where we had days with the kids. I wouldn't want them in day care every day. That's something we never had to face."

"You would have worked through it," Elizabeth re-assured him.

"Yeah. She was always there, just like Max. We would have found a way to solve the problem." He frowned. "We were both domineering individuals."

"No," she said as if shocked by what he said.

"Yes," he replied and grinned. His grin faded. "We were arguing that night she was killed."

Elizabeth was surprised he brought up the subject. "You don't have to tell me," she began.

"I want you to know," he replied. "It was something trivial that had to do with my work. It was nothing important. Right in the middle of a retort I saw the car come around the curve—in my lane."

His voice lowered, filling with pain as he relived those moments. "I swerved, trying to avoid it. The car lost its traction and we went off the edge of the road. The ditch was only about six feet, but we hit it just right that we rolled."

"Oh, Rand," she whispered, her anguish for him evident in her voice.

"She screamed. It's funny that I remember that over everything else. I don't know how many times we rolled before we hit the tree. I just remember her scream and how it was abruptly cut off. I couldn't reach her because I was pinned."

He choked up. "She hung there in her seat belt. I didn't know if she was alive or dead. But I couldn't get to her."

Tears filled Elizabeth's eyes. "I'm surprised you can even get in a car," she whispered.

"That's funny, isn't it? I guess because I'm not driving, it hasn't affected me. I don't know if I could drive, since I haven't had to. Anyway, the next thing I knew, I woke up in the hospital.

"I'm ashamed to admit I begged God to take me. You see, the doctors wouldn't tell me about Carolyn so I knew she had to be dead. And I hurt so bad. I don't think there was a place on me that didn't hurt. I never knew what mind-numbing pain meant until then."

He rubbed at his eyes, and Elizabeth wondered if he was trying to keep from crying. "I don't know what happened. I started to get better... It was just too much to handle, having to live without her. I didn't see how that would be possible."

"But you've managed."

"Day by day. I still have nightmares some nights of being trapped, unable to reach her. She's calling to me but I just lie there." He paused. "Do you know, I can't sleep wrapped up in my sheets without feeling trapped."

"You just have to take it one day at a time. I know how trite that sounds, but there's no other way to deal with grief." She leaned back on the couch and stared into space. A moment later she said softly, "After the shock of being told I'd never have children, I thought I'd die. But I didn't. I had good days and bad days. Eventually, it got to where I could function again."

"Just like I have learned lately."

"Yes. And it gets easier. I've never forgotten dreams of having my own children. But I've learned to go on and live."

"I suppose," Rand said.

"Is it still too much to handle?" Elizabeth asked, planning on making a point to him.

"Some days," he replied.

"If you would lean on God, let Him help you, those days would be much easier." Elizabeth reached out and took his hand. She didn't know how else to tell him to let go of his grief except simply to say, let go.

"I just can't. Maybe soon," he added when Elizabeth squeezed his hand. "Give me a little more time."

Since that was the most encouraging thing he had said, she decided not to push it. "You know, I thought the grief would tear me apart when I finally went to God and told Him how much I hurt over the infertility and broken engagement."

"Your engagement?"

"Yeah. I had wanted a happy marriage just like anyone else. It devastated me to fail, no matter why the failure."

"Did you ever get over Michael?" he asked seriously.

She smiled. "As a matter of fact, yes. But not the way you're thinking. I was over the love long before I finally broke it off. The pain and betrayal took longer."

"What helped you get over it?"

She smiled and intertwined her fingers with his. "Someone pointed out that I was hiding behind my pain and fears. I realized I was refusing to date or even risk contact with men on a personal level because I was letting Michael control me. It took going out on an actual date to let the healing balm flow over my soul and teach me that life is too precious to waste on worries and fears."

"Elizabeth, I didn't realize," he said, grasping that she meant the date they had gone out on.

"Didn't you?"

"Not on a conscious level. I don't know what I said—"

"It doesn't matter. It woke me up."

Rand looked overwhelmed. Finally, he released her hand and opened his arms. "Come here."

She went willingly. "I wasn't sure if you would talk about your wife to me, I mean really talk. I was afraid the feelings and memories would be too personal, but over and over again you have opened up about her. I appreciate your confidences."

"You have a right to know."

"No, Rand."

"Do *not* argue that I am only a patient and you a therapist again or I will have to launch a very loud protest."

She laughed. Slowly, the laughter faded and she allowed him to hold her. Each accepted the other's presence for what it was, a simple comfort, a sharing of past pains and the beginning of healing. Finally, after what seemed like hours, Elizabeth pulled away. "Where do we go from here?"

"I don't know," Rand said. She could hear the confusion and struggle in his voice.

"Will you come to church with me?"

"Yes. No. I don't know. Things are changing so fast, Lizabeth. Let me think on it."

"That's all I ask."

He kissed her lips and then pulled back, a tender expression on his face that brought new tears to her eyes. "I think I'd better go upstairs now. I'll see you in the morning, one way or another," he added, referring to church.

Elizabeth smiled. "Either way, I'll be looking forward to it."

Chapter Eighteen

Elizabeth looked at her watch. It was time to go and Rand hadn't shown up at her door yet. Oh, well, he'd only said he'd consider going with her. She went into her bedroom and grabbed her purse and Bible, taking a little time to brush her hair and apply a fresh coat of lipstick. She didn't like to wear makeup, but made the exception when she was going to be out in public or to church.

She started down the steps and stopped in delighted surprise when Rand was already at the bottom of the stairs waiting for her.

He looked ill at ease, and before she could say anything he blurted out, "I guess it won't matter one way or the other if I go with you."

"Are you ready to go?" she asked.

"As ready as I'll ever be." He sounded doomed.

She laughed. "Relax, Rand. If you're worried about going to your church where everyone will know you, we can go to my old church."

Rand looked relieved. "Would you mind? I mean, I

agreed to go, but I just don't know if I'm up to facing all of those people yet.''

Elizabeth took his hand. "I don't mind in the least. My church is similar to yours, only much smaller. I think you'll like it there.''

She led him out to her little red sports car. As he got in, he said, "Why did I not know about this expensive car before?''

She laughed. "What gave it away?''

"Maybe the fact that I almost have to crawl into it.''

"My one indulgence. I wanted a small fun car and saved forever to get it.''

The ride to church was quick. When they entered the foyer they were greeted by several people who evidently knew Elizabeth. No one was rude, all were very polite when talking to him, but it didn't ease his tension at facing people he didn't know.

"I don't see Kaitland," Elizabeth said. "She's in charge of the day-care center here. I really wanted to introduce you. I think you'd like her.''

"Setting me up, are you?" he asked, trying to sound amused.

"Of course not," she said so quickly that Rand smiled. "She's just a nice person, and a friend of mine. Come on, let's sit down.''

"In the back row?''

"In the back row," Elizabeth agreed.

The piano player began. The music was a variety of upbeat as well as slow songs. Some people clapped, others didn't. Then everyone was seated and a prayer was offered.

Rand had forgotten how relaxing being in church could be. He absorbed what the young preacher said like a sponge. His message was on David. He sermonized on how the Israelites hid from Goliath, afraid of him. Yet David, a young lad, outraged that Goliath should mock the Lord, fought this giant and won. David was a man who knew his own mind, a king, someone who loved God. He went on to say that, despite the great feats attributed to David, he was just as human as us and disobeyed God.

He could have hidden and not faced the problem, but instead, in every instance, David faced his problems and came clean with God.

David was known as a man after God's own heart. Even though he made mistakes, God still blessed him for his faithfulness.

The preacher said that sometimes we let our fears rule us, or our sins, but God is there, arms open wide, wanting to welcome us back and heal our broken hearts, just as He healed David's broken heart when he disobeyed God and took a census.

He ended the message by telling the congregation that all they had to do was come to Him and He would heal a broken heart.

If Rand hadn't known Elizabeth had planned to attend another church this morning, he would have sworn she had talked to this pastor about him.

Heal the brokenhearted.

He knew he hadn't faced everything. Hadn't that been what Max and Elizabeth had both said to him? Oh, not in those words, but that he had to face the past and let it go.

They started the altar call. Rand turned to Elizabeth. "Can we go now?"

Elizabeth smiled. "Of course. Come on. This way we'll miss all the traffic." She shifted her elbow back until Rand could grasp it, and they went out to the car.

On the way home, she studied Rand. He seemed quiet
and thoughtful. She had hoped there would be a message
there about hiding from God, something that might touch
him in some way. She mentally shrugged.

It wasn't her place to try to change him. She'd already
done too much badgering. Maybe it was best the message had been about forgiveness and healing.

Of course, now that she thought about it, maybe the
healing part would help him. She admonished herself for
worrying. But she couldn't help it. And she knew why.

She loved Rand.

Despite his pain, his surliness, his tendency to close
himself off, she loved him. And she would continue to
love him even when she left.

But she didn't plan on forgetting him. He was in for
one surprise. Elizabeth was not the type to give up once
she set her mind to something. She knew Rand had feelings for her. She would just have to trust God to wake
him up to those feelings. And when the time was right,
she would be there waiting.

A heavy burden was suddenly gone with that simple
admission. No matter how long it took, she loved Rand
and she would wait for the stubborn man to admit to his
own feelings.

"You're awfully quiet," she finally said.

"It's a nice church. The preacher seemed to believe
what he said. He wasn't pushy or condescending but said
it with love, like he's gone through some trials himself."

"Oh, he has. Many, many trials. He's a really sweet
man. You should have let me introduce you."

"Another time," he murmured absently.

They pulled into the garage when they arrived home.
Rand was preoccupied as he got out of the car.

Elizabeth grew concerned when he put out his cane

and walked off, leaving her standing there. She had never seen him in this mood.

"What do you want for lunch?" she questioned, catching up with him.

"What? Oh, I'm not very hungry right now," he replied. "I'm tired. I think I'm going to go lie down for awhile." He rubbed at his temples before he again walked off, leaving her standing by the kitchen door.

Quietly, she entered the kitchen. She kicked off her shoes, remembered she wasn't at home and scooped them up. She didn't dare leave anything in Rand's path. She went upstairs, deposited everything on her bed and slipped into a pair of shorts and a T-shirt.

Downstairs, she fixed a broccoli and cheese casserole dish and ate a lonely meal. She tided up and then watched an afternoon movie. Just when she had decided that Rand must be ill and she was going to check on him, she heard his door open.

She went to the door. Rand came across the hall to her room.

Something was different about him. She sensed it immediately, saw it in the way he glowed. Then she knew. There was a peace about him that she'd not seen in the entire time she'd been working with him.

"Can I come in?" he asked, standing at her door.

She stepped back. "Sure. I was watching *Bachelor Mother*. It just ended."

"Good movie."

"Have a seat."

He chose a chair. She sat on the edge of the sofa closest to his chair, unable to stop staring at him. "Do you want something to eat?"

"No. No."

She waited. He didn't say anything.

"Rand…"

"Elizabeth…"

"Go ahead," she said.

"No, you," he insisted.

"Oh, this is ridiculous. What's the matter? You look…" She hesitated.

"Yes?" he asked.

Finally, she blurted, "Peaceful. Am I mistaken, Rand?"

He sighed and clasped his hands, making her think she must be. Then he said, so softly she could barely hear him, "It was funny, but today in church I started thinking about David's life. He went through some pretty tough times, like when Saul tried to kill him and losing his best friend, the census and adultery. His daughter…"

He sighed again and raised his hand and rubbed at his forehead. "The pastor said something very interesting. He said that David, when he immediately realized his mistake, ran to God and God healed him."

Rand shifted in his chair. "I've been really…anxious about my future. I don't know how to explain it. I see two futures for myself and no answer to the problem either one presents." He remembered the future with Elizabeth and the one without her, and both endings. "Either one leaves me miserable. I just can't imagine a future after the accident. Do you understand? It's one huge blank. I mean, I had always known I'd marry Carolyn one day. We knew what my job would be, when we would have children. Everything was always so clear. But after the accident, I knew if I let go of the past and faced up to everything, there was no future there waiting for me. It was empty. No future I controlled, at least."

"But don't you realize, Rand, that none of us, no

matter how carefully we plan, can ever really be certain of our future?"

"Oh, yeah, I know that now. I also know that David, a man after God's own heart, despite his repeated failures and heartaches, knew when he was hurting the only smart thing to do was run to God with his broken heart and let God do the fixing."

"Oh, Rand," she whispered, tears running down her face.

"Well, I've finally admitted what a mess I've made of everything. I'm blind, that's not going to change. Even if I shut myself off, there is still going to be some sort of future, whether I can control it or not. It may be blank, but I guess I just have to trust God and let God be in control."

She leaned forward and took his hands. "I'm so happy for you."

"It's hard. You and Max were right, though. After confessing all of this, my heart feels lighter than I have ever felt, and—" he swallowed "—I don't think Carolyn blames me for her death."

He felt his tears close to the surface again, and blinked. He had never cried in front of anyone before and he wasn't about to start now.

"So, I just wanted you to know before you left that your harping paid off."

There was a hesitation, then Elizabeth said, "What about dating? Have you changed your mind about us?"

Rand dropped his head. Releasing her hand, he clasped his own between his knees. "Despite all I learned today, Elizabeth, I just can't risk loving a woman when I'm blind. It wouldn't be fair to her. She would come to resent it later on."

"Why don't you let the woman decide that?" she asked, hurt piercing her heart.

"Because women think with emotions. Men think more logically."

"What a sexist remark," Elizabeth cried, outraged, the hurt suddenly gone.

He mouth twitched as he replied, "It's the truth."

"Oh, you're impossible, Rand Stevens," she said, exasperated when she realized he was actually teasing her.

He smiled, despite the hurting in the region of his heart. "Maybe."

"Men think with their emotions, too," Elizabeth muttered. "I can think of one hardheaded mule who is doing that right now. But it's okay. He'll come around."

"What are you muttering about, Elizabeth?"

"Oh, nothing," she said sweetly as if he hadn't heard every word. "Nothing at all. If you'll excuse me, I'm hungry. If you want some supper you can come down and join me in about twenty minutes. It is, after all, almost dark out. You've been in your room all day."

She stood and started toward the door. "*Women* think with their emotions," she muttered. "Emotions. I ought to hit him over the head with a pan and let him see my emotions." She was at the stairs when he heard the remark.

Well, he had done it. He had severed his ties with Elizabeth, the person who had brought him to the place where he was finally at peace with himself and God.

Though it had hurt them both, it had been for her own good that he had broken it off.

So, why didn't he feel any better? He rubbed at his forehead, the headache increasing as he sat there and thought of Elizabeth.

Why did he feel a little check in his heart that said he was making the biggest mistake of his life?

Why did he want to run after her and tell her it was all a joke, that he really didn't mean it at all?

Why, indeed?

Chapter Nineteen

"Aw, man," Rand said, bending over and grabbing his head. His cane clattered to the floor.

Elizabeth, who had been thinking of their conversation the night before, jumped up, alarmed at Rand's actions. "What's the matter? What is it?"

"These headaches."

"*What* headaches?"

Slowly, the pain subsided. Rand lifted his head. "I've been having headaches since the accident, but nothing like this. I guess it's stress related."

She wondered what he could be so stressed out about and knew it was probably the anxiety of going out in public so much.

"Sit down," she said, taking his arm and helping him to a chair.

"I'm already better. Don't worry about it."

"Hey, that's my job," she said. She got the rarely used blood-pressure cuff and took his blood pressure. She checked his pupils. Finally, she ran through his chart.

"You say it's not as bad?"

"No. It's just sharp pains that will lance through my head and then they're gone. Sometimes they occur with light flashes, other times it's like a burst of colors. Sounds like what Carolyn used to describe as migraines."

"Except those don't last for such a short duration," Elizabeth said. Seeing how pale he was, she said, "Why don't you go upstairs and lay down. I'll bring some pain relievers up to you."

"Really, I'm fine."

"Really, I insist," she retorted. "You've been pushing yourself the last couple of weeks. It won't hurt for you to slow up for today."

He mumbled something under his breath and started toward the stairs.

Invalid was the only word Elizabeth caught.

"What was that?" she asked sweetly.

"If I'd wanted you to hear, I would have said it louder."

Elizabeth couldn't help it. She laughed.

But once Rand was out of sight she wasn't laughing. She went to the phone and called his personal physician. Rand had refused doctors' visits shortly after he got home. Anything could have developed during that time. She really needed to check with his doctor to make sure he didn't want to see Rand.

In less than a minute the man was on the phone. "I assume this isn't your weekly report, since I usually get those in writing, Elizabeth, so what's up?"

"I just found out Rand's been having some serious headaches over the past few months. I doubt he'd have mentioned them at all if I hadn't witnessed one. When I questioned him about them I got the impression they're getting worse. I wanted to ask you if you thought you should see him.''

"I doubt he'd see me,'' the doctor said, and she could hear the weary concern in his voice.

"I'll make sure he gets there if you think it's serious enough,'' Elizabeth replied, her voice ringing with authority.

The doctor chuckled. "I just bet you will. I've really enjoyed your reports. Some have been very colorful.''

"I didn't say anything in them—''

"Oh, but you did. Obstinate in his determination, and mulish, and a few other descriptive words that I can't remember right now.''

"Oh, well...'' She changed the subject. "I was concerned. I know you weren't done testing him when he refused any more treatment. I thought—''

"You did right,'' the physician interrupted. "If you can get him in, I'd like to see him in the morning. You know,'' he said, his voice bemused, "I never was able to find out what was causing his blindness. I was very upset when he wouldn't let me complete the testing. I really would appreciate a look at him. Be here about nine if you can.''

"Thank you,'' Elizabeth said and hung up the phone. Her concern was eating at her. Could there have been embedded glass that was working its way out of his scalp? He'd had a few lacerations to his head. Or maybe there was a blood clot?

She went to the kitchen and found the prescription medicine Rand had brought home from the hospital. She got a glass of water and went up the stairs.

"Rand,'' she called, going toward his bedroom. She found him sitting in a chair near the balcony door. "I brought you some medicine.''

"I don't like medication," he grumbled.

"Take it," she retorted.

He shot her a cross look and did as she said. When he was done, she sat on the footstool in front of him. "I've made an appointment with the doctor for you in the morning."

"You had no right to do that," Rand thundered. "You can just go down and cancel it."

"No."

"No?" he asked, incredulously.

She grinned at his shock. "What would you have discovered if you found bones on the moon?"

"A joke? Now? Look, Elizabeth, I don't feel like this."

"Come on, trust me. What would you have discovered?"

"I don't know. That there was life up there?"

"No." She laughed softly, triumphantly. "That the cow never made it."

"You do realize these are getting worse as you go along."

"I'll stop when you want me to."

"Really?"

She ignored the hopeful note in his words. "Do you know what I meant by that joke?"

"No."

"Sometimes there are reasons for things we don't see. They all need to be checked out. This could be something serious, like life on the moon," she joked. "Or it could be something not so serious, like the cow missing his jump."

He shook his head, a reluctant smile twitching his lips. "This is *not* a funny situation, Elizabeth."

"I know that."

"Last time, one of the doctors told me it was all in my head, that there wasn't anything really the matter. Thank you, but no. I don't want to hear that again."

Elizabeth reached out and took his fisted hand in her own hands. Slowly, his fist relaxed and his hand finally opened up. She clasped it. "The doctor was only suggesting a possibility. You did grieve over your wife."

"Who wouldn't?"

"And felt guilty over her death."

"Again, who wouldn't?"

"There are some who might not. However, in extreme cases like this it's necessary to explore all possibilities. If you were having chest pains and nothing showed up on the X ray or EKG wouldn't you want the doctor to check for stress-related problems? Or do a CAT scan to see if there was something else? You don't stop with one test. You need to explore and find out what's going on."

"Why are you so worried?" he demanded, throwing her off guard.

She came up blank for an answer.

He smiled, satisfied.

She hated that smile. She decided to be honest with him. "Because I care for you."

"Yeah, a real good therapist," he replied sardonically.

"I love you," she clarified.

The sneer left his face.

Before he could comment, she stood. "The medicine will make you sleep. Better get in bed." And she was gone.

Rand went to the bed and lay down, still in shock over what Elizabeth had just said to him.

I love you.

Well, she had pulled out all the punches, hadn't she?

Even after he had made it clear he wanted nothing more than a date or two.

But that was a lie. With her bald statement, all of his dross had been washed away to reveal the true yearning of his heart. He loved Elizabeth and wanted her very much. He didn't want just a date or two, and she had seen through that. He wanted her forever and ever. It did no use to try to push her away out of fear. Those words were never going to leave his heart.

The pain increased in Rand's head, but he didn't wince. Since he was already having an episode of pain, he could control the sudden spurt.

You've forgiven yourself, but you haven't taken that final step. Trust Me to provide for you, no matter what.

"Father, God," he whispered, suddenly realizing how dense he had been. "I've never really trusted you to lead me or guide me."

Why not take a chance with Elizabeth, he suddenly decided. He loved her and she loved him. After all, trust was a verb this time. He had to step out in order to put that trust into action. The only other choice was to hide and never risk anything again. It all boiled down to a matter of trust.

The medication started pulling him into the depths of oblivion. He had to tell Elizabeth.

He'd been such an idiot, so *blind*. If he could just talk to her, apologize for taking so long to see such a simple truth...

He felt tears in his eyes as he thought of his future. He could now see a different ending to one of the two scenarios. The one with Elizabeth as his wife. He could step out in trust and faith. Yes, he risked heartache. But there was a greater risk, that he just might find Elizabeth could love him as he was.

"You would have liked her, Carolyn," he whispered. Feeling a peace flood him, he finally smiled and allowed the medication to take action and lull him into a dreamless sleep where the pain was no longer.

Rand awoke feeling better than he had in months. Touching the bedside clock, he realized it was late, way past ten. And Elizabeth was usually in bed by eleven.

He sat up in bed, little aftereffects of the drug remaining in his system. He thought about changing but was in a hurry to get downstairs and find Elizabeth. He was nervous but determined to talk to her tonight. Now that he had made his decision about how he felt, there was no reason for either of them to go through more torture.

Going down the stairs with a jaunty step, he called out before he had even reached the ground floor. "Elizabeth?"

Just as he reached the bottom step he heard the library door open. "Elizabeth?" he said, turning toward her.

"I was…reading."

His steps slowed. A curious smile on his face, he said, "I didn't realize you enjoyed reading."

"Yes. Yes, I do."

Something wasn't right. Her voice sounded strained. "What is it, Elizabeth?"

"Nothing."

"Elizabeth?" he asked. "I hear it in your voice."

She let out a shaky breath. Alarmed, he strode toward her.

"More pictures arrived today."

"Again?" he asked, surprised. Reaching out, Rand took her arm and guided her into the room. "I'll call the lawyer. Maybe he has traced whoever has been doing this."

When Elizabeth didn't comment, Rand turned her toward him. Touching her face with his right hand, he frowned. "You've been crying."

"These pictures are a little different. I think you'd better sit down."

"You're only causing my blood pressure to go up by delaying it, Elizabeth. Tell me what's different."

She tried to pull away, but he wouldn't let go of her. He walked with her to the desk. "They're a set of the same pictures, but, Rand, these have been destroyed."

"Destroyed? How?" He reached out for them and felt what she was talking about even as she explained.

"The person took a pair of scissors to them. They've been cut to ribbons. And, Rand, in each picture, we've been decapitated."

He dropped the pictures like they were poison. "That's it. I'm calling the police, now."

"There's something else."

He paused in the act of lifting the phone to his ear. "What else?"

"There was a note this time. It says simply, *You're mine.*"

Rand put the phone to his ear even as he said, "That doesn't make any sense. If my lawyer had been getting obsessive letters like that, he would have told me."

A sudden frown marred his brow when he realized there was no dial tone.

"I was thinking. Rand?"

"What?" he asked, clicking the hang-up button to get a tone.

"Maybe it's not you they're after."

He paused, lowering the phone slightly and turning toward Elizabeth, his blood slowly turning to ice.

"I was thinking. Well, maybe it's me. Maybe my past has finally caught up with me again."

Rand opened his mouth to reply.

The lights in the house went out.

Chapter Twenty

❧

"Rand! The lights just went out."

"There's no dial tone, either. Go up to my room and get the cellular. Then lock yourself in the bathroom."

"What about you?"

"I'm going to check the doors. I'll be right up."

"Rand! I don't want to leave you—"

"Do it!" His harsh command left no room for argument.

He heard her hurry toward the stairs. Immediately he went to the front door and locked it. Running through the house as quietly and safely as possible, he reached the back door and snapped the lock home. He had the pool door, the back balcony door and the garage door left. Heading toward the pool door, he stopped to get the garage door.

Glass broke upstairs.

Rand's blood turned cold. It had only been thirty seconds, maybe less, since he'd sent Elizabeth upstairs. He wondered if she'd had time to get his phone and get in the bathroom.

He turned and at a dead run he reached the doorway to the living room.

Elizabeth's scream rent the air.

Blood pounded in Rand's ears. *Not Elizabeth, God. Please, not Elizabeth, too.*

As he sprinted up the stairs, every possible encounter went through Rand's mind. Elizabeth in the hands of a maniac. Elizabeth fighting with a thief. Elizabeth with Michael.

The detective had called only two days ago saying Michael had gotten out of prison and had a job. But every few months it appeared he had drifted to something else. Rand hadn't told Elizabeth because he hadn't seen any reason. The detective had traced Michael's whereabouts to one month ago. He was supposed to be checking out a source and had promised to call him back by tomorrow.

Please, don't let it be Michael. Out of all the possibilities, that one scared him the most.

Just as he got to his room, Rand heard a muffled thud and another cry of distress from Elizabeth. He went bounding in, slowing only as he approached the bedroom where he'd heard the sound.

"Come on in, Mr. Stevens."

The voice sounded gritty, sandy, filled with hate. He debated going in. He knew he couldn't leave Elizabeth in there alone, but there had to be something he could do. Then he realized Elizabeth had said the lights were out. That would be a definite plus on his side. He heard Elizabeth struggle again and then she cried out. "I said get in here. And I want to hear you talking. There's no moon out tonight."

"I'm here," Rand said, walking slowly into the room. "Let Elizabeth go."

He laughed. "Excuse me, Mr. Stevens, for laughing. But you sounded just a little possessive there. I don't think I like that."

"Who are you?" he asked, though he already knew.

"It doesn't matter," the man replied. "All that matters is the little lady has decided to come with me."

"Is that true, Elizabeth?"

There was a hesitation then the man snapped, "Answer him."

He heard her cry out.

"Never did like me to pull your hair, did you? Is that why you cut it all off first chance you got? There'll be no more of that."

"Elizabeth?"

"Yes, Rand. I want to go with him. He has a gun…" Her sentence ended in a whimper.

"He didn't ask about my gun, honey."

Rand pictured the man caressing Elizabeth's cheek as he said it. The absolute terror in her whimpers suggested he was right. He wondered what Michael had done to her before he'd arrived. Was she hurt anywhere? Did he dare ask? He inched forward, expecting Michael to cry out for him to stop at any second. Evidently, with no moon and any starlight coming from behind him, Michael could not see him.

"You know, I never would have found Elizabeth if it hadn't been for the news program I happened to see. They were doing an exposé on you and your brother. The great Stevens brothers and their success in the business world. They speculated about the new woman in your lives. Imagine my surprise when it was my fiancée's face they flashed on the screen."

"Ex-fiancée," Rand corrected, then inched closer. He followed the sound of Michael's voice. Elizabeth's ex-fiancé was evidently standing just shy of the nightstand near the chair. If he could hit them just right, maybe Elizabeth could escape.

"Well, now, that's debatable," Michael said. "I never agreed to the breakup. She'd be my wife now if she hadn't run off. But that doesn't matter. You heard it from her own lips. She wants to go with me."

"Only someone drugged and incoherent would want to go with you," Rand said, whispering a prayer even as he provoked the lunatic before him. "And I'm warning you, Michael. If you try to take Elizabeth out of this house at gunpoint I'll see you locked up for the rest of your life."

Michael laughed, an ugly sound full of triumph. "You're blind. Your threats somehow just don't carry much weight."

Done talking, Michael jerked Elizabeth. "Come on."

Rand heard Elizabeth whimper and then pull back, bumping the nightstand. "No! I won't!"

That was his chance. Michael would surely be distracted.

Rand lunged.

Three bodies went down. "Run, Elizabeth!" Rand yelled even as her soft body wiggled away. "Call the police."

Rand's hand found the gun by luck or divine guidance, he wasn't sure which.

The man under him swung, catching Rand in the chin. Rand kneed him, which caused another round of cursing. But Michael didn't let go of the pistol.

Suddenly, a shot rang out, then a second and third. "I'll kill you both!" Michael panted.

Rand gained his knees and with a jerk managed to wrestle the gun away. He threw it toward the other room.

Michael, losing some of his courage without the gun, stood and turned toward the balcony door. Rand grabbed him, refusing to let this man get away until the police got there.

Michael had other ideas.

He swung around, and Rand felt the momentum of his swing. He ducked and brought his fist into Michael's gut.

Michael staggered from the blow, which was filled with rage. Rand lunged forward but his hands only met with air.

Michael's cry as he went over the balcony was suddenly cut off by a dull thud.

Rand stood there, his adrenaline surging as he opened and closed his fist. Pain shot through his skull. He grabbed at the sides of his head even as he turned and called Elizabeth's name. "Where are you? Michael went over the balcony. I don't think..."

Bright lights flared behind his eyes, knocking him to his knees. Heaven help him, he felt like his head was going to split in two. The pain seemed to last forever as bright lights swirled in a kaleidoscope before him. Slowly, the colors dimmed and faded. Drained, Rand struggled back up. "Elizabeth..."

His voice trailed off in sudden confusion.

He was seeing things. Or was he imagining it? Had he been shot? He checked everywhere, then realized he could see himself, as well.

Everything was blurry and very dark. Of course, it was very dark in here.

"Elizabeth!" he shouted, unsure whether to be excited or terrified. He couldn't see. It was impossible. But... He started forward and stumbled over something in the floor.

Looking down, he saw the shape of a body.

His heart quit beating.

"Elizabeth?" he questioned, falling to her side.

He saw the pale redheaded woman lying so still. A face he'd never seen before, yet... He touched the softly contoured features and immediately knew this was his Elizabeth.

"God, please, no!" He started searching her for any injury. It was when he touched her stomach that his hand came away bloody.

Chapter Twenty-One

Max came rushing into the hospital and looked around, desperate to find his brother. When he'd arrived home only a few minutes ago he'd found the police there, but no one else. Evidently Elizabeth had been shot by her ex-fiancé, who was in surgery at one of the local hospitals, and Rand had gone in the ambulance with Elizabeth.

His steps slowed as he approached the surgery area. Rand was sitting there. "Rand?" he said, seeing his brother's hands and shirt covered in red splashes of what he guessed to be Elizabeth's blood. "Are you okay?"

Rand's head jerked up and his eyes squinted in Max's direction. Max stopped and blinked.

"Rand?" he asked moving toward him and watching as Rand followed his progress. Suddenly his knees turned to jelly and he staggered. "I— Are you— Can you *see* me?"

Rand sighed, a long, broken sound. "I don't know how it happened. Everything is still sort of blurry but I can see shapes, and enough of your face to know it's you."

"Rand, that's great!" Max pulled Rand from his seat, grasping his brother in a bear hug.

"Is it?" he asked.

Max let go of Rand. Rand sat down and dropped his head into his hands. "Practically the first sight I saw was Elizabeth covered in blood."

"I'm so sorry," Max whispered fervently in his Cajun accent. "How is she?"

"I don't know. Michael broke in. I had sent her upstairs to get the cellular while I locked up everything. Michael came in through the balcony doors to my room. I managed to get Elizabeth away from him, and struggled until I got the gun. Three shots went off in the process. He fell off the balcony. I was so relieved that Elizabeth was okay. She had gone to call the police.

"I didn't even know she was injured until I tripped over her. I was so busy staring at my hands... I got some of my vision back right after the fight, you see."

"She'll be okay, Rand."

"She's got beautiful hair, and her skin is so white. The colors there... But the blood is all I can see right now. I felt a wet spot and held my hand up. God help me, I thought I was going to throw up when I saw it."

Rand's shoulders slumped. "I just couldn't protect her."

"Rand!" Max said, truly shocked. "The police told me Michael would have killed her if you'd not stopped him."

"You don't know that," Rand said. "Maybe he just had the gun to scare her into coming back to him, though I sure didn't believe that at the time."

"No, Rand. You're so wrong," Max informed him,

his voice grave. "They found your detective at a hotel in Baton Rouge. The police were still at the house when I got there. Evidently, the man you hired to hunt down Michael found out where Michael was staying and confronted him there—dead."

"What!" Rand asked, horror creeping across his features.

"Yeah, bro. Had you not stopped him, Elizabeth would surely be dead, too. At least now she has a fighting chance."

"I can't lose her, Max." The low, tortured voice barely sounded like the confident Rand of the past few weeks. Max reached out and gently punched Rand on the leg.

"We won't let that happen."

"We can't stop it," Rand said. "If nothing else, over the last year and a half I have learned that we have no control over the future."

"You love her."

"Yeah. I love her. She's taught me so much, not just about being blind... Man I can't believe I can see," Rand said as if he was still just coming to grips with that. "Elizabeth would want to know. She'd want to know that because of her patience and enduring strength I finally realized it doesn't matter if I'm blind or not. I was coming downstairs to tell her I loved her and wanted to marry her when the lights went out."

"You have prayer, Rand. If you just trust God—"

"I've already got that part of my life straightened out."

Max's eyes showed his visible relief. "Then what are you waiting for? If I were you and had no hope left, I think I would be praying. Which I think I'll do, too. After all, Elizabeth will be a wonderful sister-in-law."

Rand bowed his head. His heart ached with the pain and fear. Tears filled and spilled over his eyes. *Please, God,* he said silently. *Please, God, please, God, please, God.* Though it wasn't much of a prayer, he knew God saw what was in his heart, the needs he couldn't find the words to articulate.

And then, as if in answer to his simple prayer of petition, he saw a flash of green pants as the surgeon came walking toward them. Rand stood, tapping Max, who had been praying, too.

His heart in his throat, Rand stared at the doctor. He felt Max's arm go around him for support.

"She's going to be okay."

Rand was certain he was going to pass out. He fell into his chair, joy surging inside him even as new tears fell.

"The spleen was hit, a couple of other areas of damage as the bullet tore through her. We patched her up. She's in ICU and will be there a few days. But I suspect within a week or so she'll be ready to go home."

"Thank you, Doctor." *Thank you, God.*

Rand shook his hand then turned and in a surprising display of affection hugged his brother, slapping him on the back in his enthusiasm.

"If one of you wants to see her, I'm sure it'd be okay, but just for a couple of minutes."

Rand looked at Max.

"Go on," Max said. "She'll be glad to see you."

Rand didn't wait. He took off down the hall. He was directed to her cubicle and quietly slipped inside.

She looked pale. He squinted, trying to bring her into focus. Careful of all the monitors, he went to the rail of her bed and looked at her.

Her eyes were closed, dark lashes so still against her

pale cheeks that at first he thought the doctor had lied. He glanced at the heart monitor and saw it bleeping. Reassured, he looked down. She was so small and frail...and beautiful.

He reached out and took her hand. A soft sigh escaped her lips, and then she blinked. Looking up fuzzily, she smiled. "Rand?"

"Yeah, darling, it's me."

"Oh, you can see," she said, so matter-of-fact that Rand blinked twice before he realized she must be so drugged she didn't realize what she was saying.

"Yeah, honey, I can. You're beautiful."

"I'm ugly...and fat. They've put me in with the hippos."

Rand smiled, having heard all about his own crazy comments the many different times he'd been recovering from the effects of anesthesia. "I'll take you out of the hippos, honey. Don't worry."

"Will you? I want to be with you instead."

"Yeah, honey. I love you."

"I love you, too, Rand," she said so sweetly that his heart felt as if it would explode with pride. This woman loved him. He still couldn't believe he had a second chance at life, and with this woman. It was too much to hope for, but he had it, and his sight, as well.

He didn't deserve it. But that didn't stop him from grabbing hold of it and taking the chance. Elizabeth didn't have to hit him with a two-by-four to make him understand, although it had been close there. Realizing he was giddy with relief, he reined himself in. Leaning down, he gently lifted her hand and placed a kiss on her palm. "I can't stay, but I wanted to make sure you had good dreams while I wasn't here."

"Oh, no," she whispered. "You don't mean you're going to put me in with the chickens."

He laughed. "No, honey. I'm going to keep you with me. I want you to dream about where and when you'd like to marry me. Think on that while you sleep. We'll discuss it when you get better."

"You promise, Rand? I don't want you hiding from me again."

He reached out and gently stroked her cheek. "I promise, Elizabeth."

Epilogue

Elizabeth paced the small room, wringing her hands in time with her steps. "Thank goodness," she cried when Max walked in. "I didn't think you were coming."

"And miss walking you down the aisle?"

"You're also Rand's best man. I was afraid he had chickened out at the last minute."

"Chickened?" He laughed. "Leave it to you to use that word. After all Rand has told me, I would think those jokes of yours would be the one thing that might have driven him away. But no fear. He's out there, and not nearly as nervous as you."

"He's not?" She sounded suddenly miffed. Throwing her veil over her shoulder, she shrugged. "Well, I'm not nervous anymore. It's just that you were supposed to be here fifteen minutes ago!"

"Rand got a call. He wanted me to tell you that your ex is going to end up getting life. He thought you'd want to know."

Elizabeth smiled. "I suppose. Is Rand wearing his contacts?" she suddenly asked, and went back to pacing.

"You know how stubborn he can be. I mean, he's not sure if he even wants to attempt the surgery that can correct his vision. As a matter of fact, he joked and told me he wasn't going to wear the contacts but carry his cane..."

"He was only kidding."

"Well," Elizabeth muttered, not slowing her pace as she careened around Max, "I'm not used to this new Rand that jokes and laughs all the time." She made a huffing sound then mumbled, "He shouldn't joke when I don't know it."

Max laughed. "Well, dear," he said, looking at his watch, "I think he won't be in a joking mood if we don't get you down that aisle in the next two minutes."

Elizabeth came to an abrupt halt. "Now?" she whispered, and Max was certain she paled.

"Yeah. Are you ready?"

She nodded.

Max vowed right then never to marry. If this was what a groom and bride went through, he didn't want to experience it. Rand had been just as bad until he'd stepped into the church. When Max had left him to come to Elizabeth's side, Rand had been wearing a silly grin and laughing at nothing in general.

It was scary.

The music started, and Max stepped out of the back room and into the church.

It was a beautiful day for a wedding, Rand thought, watching his bride come down the aisle on his brother's arm. And Elizabeth would notice that as soon as she came out of her shock.

He'd had to propose to her twelve times before she remembered it. He supposed he should have waited until she was out from under the effects of all the pain relievers. But it had been worth it to see her sweet smile and eager acceptance each time.

You wouldn't know how eager she'd been, looking at her now. She looked as if she was walking to her death. He never would have believed his outgoing, boisterous little redhead could get stage fright.

Of course, with over seven hundred guests, he imagined it might be a little overwhelming.

Max stopped by his side and placed Elizabeth's ice cold hand in Rand's, beaming proudly. Rand wanted to roll his eyes. Max acted as if he were the father of the bride giving away his daughter.

"Elizabeth," Rand whispered when the preacher opened his book and prepared to read his notes.

She smiled at him, but her eyes were wide and her smile was stiff.

He grinned. He knew he shouldn't do it, but he just had to get that look off her face. Besides, weren't weddings supposed to be memorable? "Elizabeth, honey, why'd the rooster cross the road?"

Well, the glazed look was gone. She glanced over her shoulder at the guests then looked at him as if he'd grown two heads. "Now, Rand?" she asked, then said, louder, "*Not now.*"

He nodded, a devilish grin spreading across his face.

"Are you ready?" the pastor asked.

"Come on, Elizabeth," Rand cajoled. "I won't allow the pastor to proceed until you answer my question."

The pastor looked a little nonplussed and then crossed his hands and waited.

"I'm going to kill you, Rand," she said, color returning to her face as she blushed.

"Elizabeth," Rand drawled. "Why'd the rooster cross the road?"

"I don't know!" Her voice rose. She squelched it, glancing again over her shoulder to see if she had been overheard. "Fine, Rand. Why did the rooster cross the road?" Her incredulity that he would hold up the wedding to retaliate with a joke showed plainly on her face.

With a triumphant smile, Rand replied, "Why, to marry his wonderful chick."

Elizabeth's eyes widened. There was a moment of complete silence as she absorbed his wisecrack.

Later, the pastor would say the Rand and Elizabeth Stevens wedding was the first he'd ever performed where the bride broke into gales of laughter before the ceremony had even started.

* * * * *

Acknowledgments

Thanks to my critique partner, Yvonne Grapes, as well as my Genie and Birt friends! Thanks Sharon Gillenwater for her gentle words and suggestions. And to my own "Phil-ton" aka Phil Hayward—a great friend. Especially thanks to my husband, Steve, and two children, Christina and Jeremiah, for all the chicken jokes!

And thanks to my mom, Helen, and in memory of my dad, Leo Weaver, who always believed in me. I love you.

Dear Reader,

When I came up with the idea for a blind hero, I wanted to tell a story we all could relate to. I think that's why I showed Rand retreating from the world. Emotional pain as well as physical blindness can often cause us to pull away from people and look inward, instead of outward to God for help. I needed a heroine who could force Rand to stop focusing inward and look outward instead. After all, doesn't the Bible say that's where our help comes from? Him? And God always teaches each of us differently. So I thought, how about a zany, nutty woman who tells awful jokes over and over. And what type of jokes? The kind you absolutely hate to hear from your kids when they come home from school and say, "Hey, Mom, guess what I heard…" Using her jokes to break through Rand's inward concentration and teach him that there are other answers—not always the same ones we think of—was Elizabeth's special method.

So, I sat down to write and found I had more fun with this book than anything else I'd ever written. Of course, my family groaned every time I asked, "Okay, tell me another one." But I think they secretly enjoyed the fun time we had together coming up with chicken jokes.

However, despite Elizabeth's lighthearted side, I knew the story wouldn't be complete unless she too were facing some unnamed fear. And it had to be something that Rand could solve for her only if he learned the lessons Elizabeth had been trying to teach him. So, my gothic streak added a stalker to the story.

I hope you enjoyed the results.

God Bless,

Cheryl Wolverton

Coming in March 1998, from Love
Inspired, the story of the Stevens brothers
continues with Cheryl Wolverton's
A FATHER'S LOVE.

Millionaire bachelor Max Stevens finds twin babies abandoned on his doorstep and life is never the same again. The adorable tots reunite Max with the one woman in his past he could never forget. But can Max now learn to open his heart—and forgive?

Just turn the page for an exciting preview....

Chapter One

The cries woke him.

Multi-millionaire bachelor Max Stevens rolled over in his bed and listened to the sounds that drifted to him on the early morning breeze through the open balcony doors.

It couldn't be the television, since his brother, Rand, and his new wife, Elizabeth, were on an extended honeymoon. Besides, the sounds wouldn't reach here to his suite of rooms.

None of the staff at the house he shared with his brother would dare turn a TV on while on duty. Gauging from the pale light outside the doors it was probably 6:00 a.m.

Max pushed himself up in bed, the silk sheet sliding down his bare chest and pooling at his waist.

Swinging his bare legs over the edge of the bed, he slid his feet into slippers and grabbed his silk robe, shrugging it on over his paisley shorts.

He rubbed a weary hand over his face as he strode to the balcony door. This was not how he liked to be awakened early in the morning. He had a hard day of work ahead of him and it would've been nice to have been done with his morning devotions and prayer *before* this interruption. His whole day would be off-kilter now.

Padding down the balcony stairs, Max followed the wrought-iron railing around the curve to the patio below. But when he turned the corner he stopped in stunned amazement and stared.

"Sarah!" It was his housekeeper's doing. It had to be. "Sarah, where are you!"

He continued to stare, rooted to the spot until he heard the hurried footsteps of his housekeeper. "Oh, mercy me."

Her gasp told him he'd been wrong. "Are these yours?"

"Certainly not."

"Well, do something," he finally said.

"Like what?" she asked.

He realized she didn't have any idea what to do or was too amazed to do it. "You're a woman. Don't you know how to handle these things?"

"That's a sexist remark, Mr. Stevens."

Realizing she didn't intend to move from her position as an observer, he stepped forward. The sounds stopped. He raised an eyebrow.

"Well?" Sarah prodded.

He shot her a look that told her to mind her tongue and took another step forward. "They are small, aren't they?"

"I guess. But you would know better than me."

He glanced over his shoulder. "And what do you mean by that?"

Sarah had been with the household since both Max and Rand were boys so Max's scowl didn't faze her in the least. Plopping her hands on her ample hips, she replied, ''What do you think I mean? They look just like…look, there's a note.''

Max plucked the piece of paper off the side of the basket and began to read:

Dear Max,
I had no one else to leave them with. I'm in trouble, and have to leave. I know you'll take care of them and love them for me. Please don't tell anyone the secret. I've always thought they looked like my knight in shining armor. I've never forgotten you. Thank you. You're a kind man.

P.S. Meet Maxwell Robert and Madeline Renee.

Max stared in disbelief at the note until a gurgle from the basket drew his attention.

Maxwell and Madeline?

Two cherubic faces no more than a year or so old stared back at him. He wasn't sure how old they were but knew they were too big to have just been born. And the writer of the note was right. They both had dark hair and one's eyes were changing to a deep brown accentuating a Cajun lineage.

But his?

Impossible! He knew that for certain.

''Well, Mr. Stevens,'' Sarah huffed, her voice reeking with disapproval. ''Are you just going to leave your kids here on the porch or bring them into the house?'' She pivoted and marched away before he could answer.

His kids.

Dear Father, he thought, staring at the two children who were beginning to squirm against the bonds that held the back of their overalls to the handles of the basket. *I know these aren't my kids. I know it. So, would you mind telling me what I'm getting myself into this time?*

God didn't answer.

Max took that to mean he would find out in time. Inching forward, not sure if his nearness would set the kids off, he picked up the two bulky, blue-and-pink-striped bags and the laundry basket that held the two tiny children.

The one with the brown eyes, he thought it was the girl since she had a pink ribbon in her hair, gurgled and kicked her feet.

The other one chewed on his toe and studied Max with a serious expression.

"Well, uh, kids, I don't quite understand this, but for some reason your mommy left you with me. She sounded scared in the note. But don't worry. Hopefully, she'll be back soon because…to be honest, I don't have the faintest idea what to do with you. But maybe we can get along fine until…until we get this all worked out."

The blue-eyed child frowned and released his foot, kicking Max in the nose.

Max froze, afraid they'd start crying.

The child wiggled his toes against Max's mouth as if offering him a taste.

Max grimaced and started to inch his feet toward the door, deciding the kids would be better off on the floor inside, instead of trying to jam their feet down his throat.

Maddie laughed, which caused the other child to gurgle too.

Relieved that they weren't going to throw a fit at his movements, Max hurried to the door. "I'm just going to take you inside now, and sit you down. I bet you're hungry. I am.''

He paused at the doors leading into the study that overlooked the balcony. Fumbling, he managed to get the door opened and get inside. "I'm not sure exactly what you eat.''

Suddenly, he sniffed, his nose wrinkling as his eyes narrowed suspiciously. "You're still in diapers, aren't you?'' Kicking the door closed, he juggled the basket for a firmer grip.

"We're going to have to do something about that right now,'' he said, though he wasn't sure what. Smiling in relief at the accomplishment of getting them into the house without another bout of crying, he decided maybe this baby stuff wasn't going to be so bad—except for the odor emanating from one of them.

Setting the basket down by the sofa, he hollered, "Sarah!''

Both children immediately jumped, then burst into tears. The terror any male bachelor immediately felt at the sight of such small children had been held at bay—until those shrieks. His eyes widened and he reached out and patted first one, then the other's shoulder. Yes, there was no doubt about it, he was in way over his head with this situation. He needed help. And fast.

* * * * *